Ollie looked around the back of ... saw two people silhouetted against the light from the window.

As he drew closer to them, he realized it was Mr. Le Blanc and his daughter. He remembered her being standoffish when they were there before. His brother, Lowell, had said she wasn't that way at all, but that's how she was around him.

"Look who's here." Anna nodded toward the couple.

"Mr. Le Blanc." Ollie spoke to the man while he set the chair near the window; then he glanced toward the woman. "Miss Le Blanc."

For an instant it seemed to Ollie as if she winced. But why would she wince when he spoke to her? Then her eyes lighted up with such a dazzling smile that it almost took his breath away. The warmth in that look touched something deep inside him. . . .

He must have misunderstood when he met her before. How could he have ever thought this exquisite creature was standoffish?

LENA NELSON DOOLEY is a freelance author and editor who lives with her husband in Texas. During the twenty years she has been a professional writer, she has been involved as a writer or editor on a variety of projects. She developed a seminar called "Write Right," and she hosts a writing critique group in her home. She presently works full-time as an author and editor. She has a dramatic ministry and speaking ministry that crosses denominational lines and an international Christian clowning ministry. She and her husband enjoy taking vacations in Mexico, visiting and working with missionary friends.

Books by Lena Nelson Dooley

HEARTSONG PRESENTS
HP54—Home to Her Heart
HP492—The Other Brother
HP584—His Brother's Castoff

Double Deception

Lena Nelson Dooley

Heartsong Presents

To my oldest granddaughter, Marissa Waldron, who is a joy to my heart. I will enjoy watching you grow into the beautiful woman God intends you to be. And every book is dedicated to the man who has shared his life with me since 1964, James Allan Dooley, the love of my life. The man God created to be my husband.

A note from the Author:
I love to hear from my readers! You may correspond with me by writing:

Lena Nelson Dooley
Author Relations
PO Box 719
Uhrichsville, OH 44683

ISBN 1-59310-121-X

DOUBLE DECEPTION

Our mission is to publish and distribute inspirational products offering exceptional value and biblical encouragement to the masses.

All Scripture quotations are taken from the King James Version of the Bible.

All of the characters and events in this book are fictitious. Any resemblance to actual persons, living or dead, or to actual events is purely coincidental.

PRINTED IN THE U.S.A.

one

July 1895

"This is the town." Pierre Le Blanc leaned toward Clarissa Voss, who shared the front seat of the surrey with him. A gentle breeze ruffled the fringe that decorated the roof of the carriage, bringing welcome relief from the summer heat.

"What's so special about this place?" The young woman glanced around. The town seemed nice enough, but nothing made it stand out from the others they'd visited. And they'd visited many over the years. "Oh, look. An ice cream parlor." She started to point, then remembered it wasn't polite. So many things her mother had taught her were drifting out of her life, no matter how hard she tried to hold on to them.

Pierre frowned at her. "You must remember, *Rissa*"—he emphasized the name—"that you have been here before. This is where you had that lovely ensemble made."

Clarissa looked down at the claret-colored silk. It had more ruffles and flounces than she liked, but it was one of the most fashionable dresses she had worn in a long time. It reminded her of the clothing she and her sister wore before their mother died. Barely realizing what she was doing, she picked at the ruffles on the skirt as she looked up again.

They were turning from the street that ran beside the rail-road tracks onto a thoroughfare leading through the middle of downtown Litchfield. If anyone had told her four years ago that she would go to Minnesota, she would have laughed and asked where Minnesota was. She never was good in geography, and New Orleans was so far from here—in more ways than one.

Clarissa wished for the quiet streets around their family home. It was situated far from the busy part of town, far from the French Quarter. She longed to hear the soft Southern drawl that had filled the air with a familiar melody. The farther north they moved, the more clipped the speech became. She sighed, longing to see her mother again. If only that were possible.

Pierre stopped the wagon in front of a store with a large sign emblazoned across the top story of the building. Braxton's Mercantile. Clarissa looked at the brightly colored words with fanciful letters and curlicues. Her gaze dropped to the windows filled with merchandise. All kinds of merchandise. Then her attention was drawn to the window at the far end.

The words *Dress Emporium* were painted on the glass, but they didn't obstruct the view of the window with its lacy sheer curtains held open by ruffled tiebacks. In the center of the window stood a form displaying an ensemble that included a hat. The chapeau rested on the shoulders of a beautiful, but simple, elegant gown in a lovely shade of blue, and an ostrich feather in the same hue was draped around the brim of the hat. Clarissa knew she would look good in that ensemble. She liked the simpler lines of the garment, and the color would bring out the sky blue of her eyes. She could imagine herself with her abundant black curls pulled up in an elaborate style with a long curl hanging down one side against the soft fabric of the dress. The hat would rest atop the hairstyle, and the wide brim would protect her creamy complexion from the sun. She would feel like a Southern belle again in that dress and hat—instead of what she had become.

"Is that where you had this dress made?" She glanced at the man who shared the seat with her.

Pierre looked at the store before he answered. "Yes." He climbed down from the surrey and came around to help her alight. "We told you all about the people and what transpired when we were here."

Clarissa pulled her light cape closer around her. The breeze felt cooler, and the dress bared her shoulders. The ensemble would be more appropriate for a party than day wear. "Is there any way we could buy the dress and hat displayed in the window of the Dress Emporium?" She was surprised she had the courage to voice the question running through her mind.

Pierre frowned. He jingled the coins in his pocket as if counting how many he had. He always did that when they talked about money. "I suppose it would be good business. But we won't purchase it if it's too expensive. Just try not to seem too interested. Remember—that always drives the price up."

Pierre drew Clarissa's hand through the crook of his arm, and they sauntered into the cool recesses of the mercantile. Clarissa blinked her eyes at the bright light inside. It had looked dark from the outside, but gaslights were scattered along the four walls. She was amazed by the abundance of the merchandise displayed there. They hadn't frequented a store with such a wide variety in a long time. Perhaps this wasn't such a backwater town after all. They wandered around the store and browsed through the items. Soon they reached the open doorway that led to the dress shop.

Pierre looked around the room until he spotted a tall young woman with dark brown hair piled on top of her head in an almost haphazard manner. "Good afternoon, Miss Jenson."

The woman turned toward them. "Hello, Mr. Le Blanc, Rissa. When did you get back in town?"

Pierre removed Clarissa's hand from the crook of his arm and moved closer to Miss Jenson.

Anna, Clarissa thought. *They said her name is Anna.*

"We've just arrived." He turned toward Clarissa. "Come, Rissa—say hello to Miss Jenson."

The woman held out her hand to Clarissa. "Remember, I told you to call me Anna. How lovely you look in that dress."

Clarissa took the proffered hand and gave it a dainty shake. "Yes. Thank you—Anna."

Pierre hovered near the woman. She moved away then and walked behind the counter that spread across the back of the room.

"How may I help you?"

Pierre followed her and leaned on the counter. Clarissa hated the way he flirted with almost every attractive woman they met.

"We'll be in Litchfield longer this time, and I'd rather not stay at the hotel. I want Rissa to be in a better, more homey environment. Do you have any suggestions?" He paused, and when Anna didn't say anything he continued. "Are there any good boardinghouses in town? Maybe in a quiet neighborhood?"

Anna lifted a bolt of fabric from the counter and placed it on a shelf behind her. Clarissa got the feeling she was trying to move away from Pierre. And Clarissa didn't blame her. If only she could put a lot of distance between herself and Pierre. Oh, if only Mother hadn't died.

Anna turned back around. For a moment, she looked as if she were thinking. "The only boardinghouse I know of is the one Mrs. Olson runs." She picked up another bolt of fabric and fussed with it. "When Mr. Olson died, she was left alone in a large two-story house. So she opened the boarding-house. That might meet your needs. It's on the residential side of town."

"It sounds perfect." Pierre inched down the counter closer to where Anna stood. "You've been so helpful, just as you were when we were here before."

Anna turned to place the bolt on the shelf beside the others. Clarissa walked around the room. The shop carried a lot of accessory items. She noticed a display of lacy white gloves arranged attractively on a small table.

"These are lovely." Clarissa picked up one and pulled it on her left hand. It fit perfectly.

"Olina Nilsson crocheted them." Anna glided around the end of the counter and across the room toward Clarissa. "She's staying home with her two children, and this gives her an outlet for her creative abilities." She picked up the other glove. "Here, try them both on."

Pierre had worked his way around the room to the window display. "Rissa, this dress is lovely. How do you like it?"

Before Clarissa could respond, Anna said, "I tried to get you to use that color when you were here before, but you said you weren't fond of it. I knew it would look good on you with your coloring."

Clarissa inspected the garment. White crocheted lace out-lined the neckline. "These gloves would go so well with that dress, wouldn't they—Father?" How she hated calling him that, but he insisted she use that form of address when they were in public.

Pierre looked at her from under hooded eyelids. Clarissa could tell he didn't like her hesitation, and she knew she would hear about it when they were alone, but she didn't care. She was so tired of this charade. If only it could end—but there seemed little hope of that.

He turned toward Anna and gave her a warm smile. "Do you think this would fit Rissa?"

"Yes, I made it soon after you left, and the measurements are very close to hers." Anna smoothed an imaginary wrinkle on the back of the dress.

"Then we'll take it and the hat—and the gloves."

Anna was smiling when she turned around. She led the way to the counter and started to write the sales slip while Pierre pulled his wallet from his pocket.

❧

"Anna, where do you want me to put this?" Ollie Jenson, Anna's brother, called to her as he came through the opening to the workroom, carrying a rocking chair.

"Over there by the window." She gestured toward a spot.

Ollie looked around the back of the chair and saw two people silhouetted against the light from the window. As he drew closer to them, he realized it was Mr. Le Blanc and his daughter. He remembered her being standoffish when they were there before. His brother, Lowell, had said she wasn't that way at all, but that's how she was around him.

"Look who's here." Anna nodded toward the couple.

"Mr. Le Blanc." Ollie spoke to the man while he set the chair near the window; then he glanced toward the woman. "Miss Le Blanc."

For an instant it seemed to Ollie as if she winced. But why would she wince when he spoke to her? Then her eyes lighted up with such a dazzling smile that it almost took his breath away. The warmth in that look touched something deep inside him. He should have tried to get to know her better during their previous visit.

Mr. Le Blanc had flirted shamelessly with Anna on his last trip. The first time he met her, he'd kissed her hand in a regal manner. Ollie decided he could be just as regal as Mr. Le Blanc. He looked into Rissa's eyes and gently took her hand in his. He lifted it to his lips and placed a light kiss on her fingertips. He was pleased to see a blush stain her cheeks—and relieved she didn't rebuff him. He must have misunderstood when he met her before. How could he have ever thought this exquisite creature was standoffish? Lowell was right; she was friendly and intriguing. Mr. Le Blanc's voice penetrated his thoughts.

"Anna, please join Rissa and me for dinner. We could take you to the restaurant in the hotel."

Anna looked startled. The man was asking her out. It was sure to set August Nilsson off again. August had been terribly jealous of the man on the last visit. Later, he and Anna had worked everything out, and now they were planning their wedding.

"Thank you for the kind invitation, Mr. Le Blanc." Anna stepped around a table and started rearranging the stack of gloves. "My fiancé and I will be dining with his family tonight."

Now the man looked startled. "I'm sorry. I didn't realize you were engaged."

"That's all right, Mr. Le Blanc." Anna smiled at him. "August and I have just recently decided to get married. You couldn't have known. Now let's get these items wrapped up for you."

She went to the window display and removed the hat and dress. Ollie had liked that dress ever since Anna and Gerda finished it. It would look good on Miss Le Blanc. He hoped he would have a chance to see her in it. He wished it could be when he escorted her to one of the frequent socials, but they probably wouldn't be staying long enough for that to happen. A man could hope, though.

Ollie watched Le Blanc while Anna finished the sale. Something about that man made Ollie uncomfortable. He wasn't sure what it was. He decided to make an effort to get to know the Le Blancs better, especially Rissa. He definitely didn't sense anything wrong with her.

Ollie left the shop and headed out of town to the farm. Once there he sought out Lowell, who was working in the barn. "You'll never guess who I just saw in town."

Lowell looked up from the horse he was currying. "So why don't you tell me, instead of keeping me guessing?"

He was always so serious. Ollie often told him he should take time to have more fun. Ollie picked up a currying comb and went into the stall adjoining the one where his brother was busy. He set to work on the palomino while he talked. "You remember earlier in the summer when that Le Blanc family came to town?"

"Sure." Lowell stopped and leaned his arms on the half wall that divided the enclosures. "What about them?"

"They were in the dress shop when I took the rocker to Anna." Ollie stood and looked his brother in the eyes. "I believe you're right about Miss Le Blanc. She was much friendlier today."

Lowell frowned. "What do you mean, friendlier?"

"I don't know. I had the impression she was glad to see me."

"So?"

"So you were right." Ollie returned to currying the horse. "But I don't think I like her father."

Lowell looked thoughtful. "I never did warm up to him myself. What did he do today?"

The horse stamped its hoof, and Ollie had to move to keep his own foot from being stepped on. "He asked Anna if he could take her to dinner at the hotel."

Lowell raised his brows. "That's not a good idea."

"Oh, Anna set him straight. She told him she and August are going to be married. Le Blanc didn't seem to like that a bit."

Lowell put his hands in the back pockets of his jeans. He rocked up on the balls of his feet then down again. "I never felt at ease around that man. It's too bad Rissa is kin to him. I wouldn't mind knowing her better."

Ollie didn't like what his brother said. He wanted that privilege himself. When he and Lowell were younger, they used to wrestle, trying to see who was stronger. Since becoming adults, they'd been best friends as well as brothers. But right now, Ollie wanted to punch him. Where had that thought come from? What was happening to him? Surely that little filly with the black hair and blue eyes couldn't come between them. A picture crept into his thoughts. A warm smile with twinkling eyes. Cheeks stained with a becoming blush.

This could be a real problem.

two

Soon after Ollie left the dress shop, August Nilsson arrived. Anna studied her hands for a moment before she began rearranging the items on the counter. Clarissa wondered why she appeared so nervous, then she remembered Pierre telling her August was jealous of him on their other trip. The big man looked muscular—and nice. She couldn't blame him for being jealous. Pierre was up to no good. He left one or more broken hearts in every town they exited. Even after such a short time, Clarissa liked Anna Jenson. She was glad a man like August was going to marry her. They looked good together with his blond handsomeness and her dark coloring.

"August." Anna hurried from behind the counter and took his arm when he entered. "Look who's come back to town."

The two men eyed each other for a moment, and the air crackled with tension; then August stepped forward and extended his hand. "It's good to see you, Le Blanc."

Pierre hesitated a moment, then reached out. After all, it wasn't good for his business to antagonize anyone this early in the game. He clasped August's hand and smiled. She wondered why no one besides her could tell how insincere that smile was. The only time he gave a real smile was when he was counting his ill-gotten gains. She didn't want him hurting these people. If only she could do something about it—but she hadn't even figured out a way to escape from his clutches herself. Oh, she had dreamed about it often enough. Either she escaped, or someone rescued her, but those dreams were like the fairy tales her mother used to read to her. They weren't real.

August turned toward her, and Clarissa smiled. She never wanted to use people the way Pierre did. She hoped he could see her smile was sincere.

August smiled at her warmly. "And I'm glad you're back, Rissa. Are you staying in town long?"

Pierre stepped behind her. He placed his hands on her shoulders and gripped—hard. When she tried in an unobtrusive way to pull away, he wouldn't let go. She might as well stand still. It would hurt less. But she didn't like his touching her, whether he was hurting her or not.

"Actually, we want to spend the rest of the summer here." Pierre was so close, his breath moved tendrils of her hair. It was all she could do to keep from shivering in disgust. "Maybe longer."

Anna clasped August's hand and looked up into his face. "Pierre and Rissa don't want to live in the hotel. Do you think Mrs. Olson has any vacant rooms?"

August smiled at Anna. Clarissa hoped someone would look at her like that someday, but with the way they lived their lives, it was unlikely. Her mother would roll over in her grave if she knew what Pierre had done since she died. This was not the life Mother had wanted for her daughters.

"Yes. Just yesterday a family moved out. Their house had burned, and they lived in the boardinghouse while it was rebuilt. Mrs. Olson said something at breakfast about cleaning up those rooms today. She was wondering where she would find more boarders." August turned toward Pierre. "Maybe you're the answer to her prayers."

Pierre moved around Clarissa. She was sure that last statement had made him squirm. She knew he didn't believe in prayers, but she wished she knew more about them. Before her father had died, the family attended church and had family devotions together, but she had been so young she couldn't understand much of it. Since she had been traveling with Pierre, they hadn't gone to church. They were often on the run by the time they'd stayed in a town no longer than a week.

"That's good. Nilsson, would you be so kind as to tell me how to find this boardinghouse?" Clarissa hated the sound of Pierre's voice, especially when he was trying to ingratiate himself into the society of a town.

August dropped a quick kiss on Anna's cheek, and a blush stole over her face. Clarissa remembered that before he died, her father and mother had had a relationship like the one August and Anna seemed to have. And it was the kind of relationship she wanted with a man. Not one such as her mother and Pierre had. She'd heard them arguing about the money he spent. He'd been attentive to her before they married but stopped as soon as he had the ring on her finger.

"I'll do more than that." August moved toward the door. "I can take the two of you there myself."

Pierre rented the two adjoining rooms on the second floor of the boardinghouse, then left Clarissa in her room with her carpetbag and the new ensemble they'd purchased. He said he was going to pick up her trunk. Clarissa was glad to have time away from him for awhile.

After hanging up the new dress, she opened her bag and started putting her unmentionables in the drawers of a polished oak highboy that sat beside one window. Then she turned around and surveyed her surroundings. It was so long since she'd had a room of her own in a real house. This one was large and airy. Since it was a corner room, she had windows on two sides, so light poured in between the priscilla curtains, bathing the room in golden brightness. She opened one window and drew in a breath of fresh air. Then she opened a window on the other wall, and a breeze blew through, cooling the room a bit.

When they had lived in New Orleans, Clarissa's room had been about this size, so it made her feel as though she had come home. Even the wallpaper with a soft cabbage-rose pattern resembled the paper she had chosen when she was just nine years old. The tall brass bed gleamed in the sunlight, and the plush quilt that covered it repeated the colors of the wall covering. She went to the bed and sat on the edge. The soft mattress was inviting. She had slept on the hard ground too long.

Clarissa took off her dress and petticoats and slipped into her dressing gown. Then she went back to the bed. Stretched out on top of the covers, she felt cradled in the softness. Turning on her side, she nestled her head into the down pillow. She was going to rest only a few minutes, but before long, she drifted off to sleep, dreaming about her beautiful, loving mother and the wonderful life that had disappeared like a vapor.

❧

Ever since Ollie told Lowell about seeing the Le Blancs in town, he sensed Lowell's withdrawal from him. What was the matter with the man? He'd only agreed with him. That Le Blanc gal was a prize, and he'd told Lowell so.

Lowell had always been quieter than he, but now his quietness bordered on sullenness. Ollie was tired of it. He saddled one of the horses and rode off down the road to exercise it. A buyer from the cavalry was coming in a few days, and he wanted all the horses in top form. People sought their family's ranch out because of the quality of the horses they raised. It was a good business that provided a comfortable living for the whole family.

He headed to his favorite place. The prairie grass grew tall and blew in the wind. Here and there a copse of trees provided welcome shade from the hot summer sun. And the frequent pools of shimmering water gave the horses plenty to drink. As he galloped across the prairie, his mind returned to the time when he had been in town. He could feast his eyes all day on that pretty little woman. She had been dressed in a pretty gown with ruffles and lace, but he could imagine her with her ebony hair pulled back and tied with a scarf. That's the way Anna wore hers when she was riding Buttermilk.

He wished Rissa was wearing riding clothes now and galloping beside him across the prairie. He was sure her sky blue eyes would light up, and the wind would bring out the roses in her creamy cheeks. He wondered if she knew how to ride a horse. Maybe he should ask. He could teach her anytime she wanted to learn.

He slowed the horse to a trot and turned back toward the farm. Wasn't there any reason for him to return to town?

ら

Pierre carried Clarissa's trunk upstairs and stayed in her room while she unpacked it. She wished he wouldn't. It made her uncomfortable when he was in her room. She didn't like the way his eyes slid over her body, half hidden behind his lowered eyelids. She felt somehow as if she needed a bath.

"Did you notice the variety of merchandise in Braxton's Mercantile?" He sat in the straight chair and propped his foot on the knee of his other leg.

Any minute, Clarissa expected him to lean the chair back against the wall. She hoped he would—and that the chair would slip. She knew her thoughts weren't kind, but when had he ever been kind to her? She was only a means to an end for him. A tool. A pawn.

"Yes," she answered distractedly. "It's a nice store."

"Do you realize what that means?"

She turned and looked at him. His voice betrayed an excitement she hadn't seen in him for a long time. "What?"

Pierre stood and took out a cheroot.

Clarissa frowned. "Please don't smoke in my room. It's so smelly."

He struck the match and held it to the tip of the rolled tobacco. After the smoke wreathed his head, he threw back his head and laughed. She wondered why he was so happy— besides the fact he was tormenting her with his smoke. She walked to the window and breathed in a lungful of fresh air.

He followed her and stood so close she could feel his breath on her neck. "If you weren't so valuable to me as a daughter. . ."

He left the sentence dangling, but she knew what he meant. He often hinted he found her desirable. The thought sickened her. She wasn't entirely ignorant of the ways of men and women. She cringed and moved back to finish unpacking the trunk.

He took another long draw on the thin cigar and blew the smoke toward her, then continued their conversation about the store as if he hadn't stopped. "Because of the variety of merchandise, I can tell this town has wealth. Now if we can figure out how to transfer much of it to my pockets."

Clarissa shuddered. Her heart broke for the nice people she had met. If only there were a way to stop him.

≈

Ollie pulled up at the blacksmith shop where August was plunging a horseshoe into the bucket of water to cool it. Steam hissed and shot up into the air.

August turned his face away and saw him standing in the doorway. "Ollie, what brings you here?"

"I want you to check the shoes on the horse I rode into

town." Ollie stood with his hands shoved into the front pockets of his jeans. He glanced toward the table where August kept the things that needed repair. He was thankful it was nearly empty. He wouldn't be wasting August's time.

Ollie walked farther into the shadows of the shop. "Do you know who was at the Dress Emporium this morning?"

August placed the cool horseshoe on a pile of similar pieces of metal. "I went by to see Anna earlier, and the Le Blancs were there. Is that who you're talking about?"

Ollie nodded. "How do you feel about that?"

August laid his tongs on the worktable. He pulled out a bandanna from his back pocket and mopped sweat off his face. "It's fine with me. I know I was jealous of him when he was here before, but not now." He stuffed his bandanna into his pocket. "I even took the Le Blancs over and introduced them to Mrs. Olson. They want to stay in the boardinghouse instead of the hotel this time."

Ollie was surprised. "Does that mean they'll be here awhile?" He hoped he didn't sound too eager.

August nodded. "It looks that way."

❧

"Did you two get settled in the boardinghouse?" Anna asked when Clarissa and Pierre entered the dress shop. She moved behind the counter and leaned both arms on it.

Pierre strode to the front of the counter and leaned on it too, close to Anna. "Yes, it's just what we wanted. Rissa even has a corner room. Very nice."

Anna shifted closer to the shelves lining the wall behind the counter. Clarissa didn't blame her. Pierre was much too forward. One day he would go too far.

"Is there some other way I can help you?" Anna's smile wasn't as broad as it had been earlier.

Pierre straightened and glanced around the store. "Yes, Rissa is so taken with the wonderful outfit we bought her this morning that she'd like to order four more."

Clarissa stifled a gasp. Pierre had told her he wanted to go to the store, but she assumed he meant the mercantile. He'd talked about it so much in her room. But they went into the dress shop instead, and now he was ordering her more dresses. He hadn't said a word about that before they came. She hoped he wasn't planning on using this as a way to get close to Anna again and cause trouble in her relationship with August.

"That's wonderful!" Anna exclaimed. "If you could leave Rissa with us for awhile, Gerda and I will help her choose the styles and fabrics that would best suit her."

Clarissa knew Pierre didn't want to leave her there alone, but she was glad. She'd like to spend part of the afternoon with the two women without him hovering over her. It had been a long time since she'd visited with other young women. After Pierre left, Anna took her into the workroom.

"Gerda, look who's come back." Anna moved around Clarissa. "You remember Rissa Le Blanc, don't you?"

"Rissa, how nice to see you again." Gerda, the seamstress, had a beautiful face and pale blond hair. "Will you be in town long?"

Clarissa felt shy around the woman. What was she supposed to know about her? Maybe Pierre hadn't told her everything. "I think we'll be here awhile."

"They're staying at the boardinghouse." Anna sat on the chair by the sewing machine. "Her father wants us to make four new dresses for her."

"That's very nice," Gerda said, smiling.

Clarissa could understand her delight. When Pierre was there before, he'd ordered four ensembles. That would make eight from this one shop. Even though he spent money in each town, he seldom established a strong relationship with any one business.

❧

No one was in the front room of the Dress Emporium when Ollie entered, but the bell above the door announced his arrival. Gerda quickly came through the curtain that covered the opening to the workroom. There was a door, but Gerda and Anna didn't like to shut it during business hours. They also didn't want everyone seeing into the workroom, so just last week he had helped them hang the curtain.

"What can I do for you, Ollie?"

"Is Anna here?" He always felt a little out of place in a woman's shop.

"Sure. Come on back."

He followed Gerda into the workroom, and there, by one of the windows, Rissa Le Blanc stood bathed in a golden glow. The light gave tiny blue highlights to her coal black hair. And her smiling eyes sparked fire in his heart. Something in this woman called to something deep within him, and it took his breath away.

❧

Clarissa returned to her room after she and Pierre ate dinner in the boardinghouse. She was glad to be alone. She wanted to revisit the events of her day, in particular the time she'd spent in the dress shop with Anna, Gerda, and Ollie. Especially Ollie.

He stayed a long time, and the four of them talked and laughed like old friends. She didn't have any friends, but she was sure that was what it felt like. Litchfield seemed to be the home she had hoped for, a place where she could belong. Where she could be accepted for who she was. But these people had no idea who she was, and she wasn't about to tell them.

If they ever found out, it would be over. The friendship—and everything else.

She paced back and forth in the room, wringing her hands. She had to stop Pierre, but how? She couldn't allow him to hurt these people as he had so many others. Just how long had this been going on? She usually tried to forget, but tonight she remembered.

She and her sister had been happy when they lived on the plantation with her mother and father. It was a wonder the family had held on to the plantation through the War between the States, but they had. After the war, her grandfather struggled to make ends meet. When her mother and father married, her father helped her grandfather try to turn the plantation around.

Her father died when she was only six years old, and her mother couldn't take care of the property. Then, with her father gone, her grandfather had sold the property and used the money to buy the house in New Orleans. There her mother met and married Pierre. Her wedding day was the beginning of the prison in which Clarissa now found herself.

She wished she were a man. If she were a man, she could stop Pierre, but what could a young woman do? Since he was her guardian, he had the law on his side. Of course he wouldn't have it if anyone ever found out about his illegal activities. She wished she had enough courage to tell someone, but Pierre had threatened her and her sister. Mari wasn't as strong as she was, so Clarissa knew she had to protect her.

Clarissa wanted to be friends with Anna, August, Gerda, and Ollie. Maybe she should just enjoy what she had as long as it lasted. It would end soon enough.

three

Lowell let out his breath and frowned. Every time he needed help, Ollie was missing. Then later he would return from town. When Lowell asked him what he was doing in Litchfield, Ollie said he went to get something repaired then visited the Dress Emporium. Their father had asked them to check on Anna, but since she'd become engaged, August was at the store often enough to keep her safe. She didn't need Ollie almost every day.

"Where have you been?" Lowell asked Ollie this time as he rode into the barnyard. "You didn't go to town again, did you?"

Ollie didn't say anything, but Lowell wasn't going to let him off the hook. They had a horse farm to run, and he couldn't do it by himself.

Finally, Ollie spoke. "Yeah, I was in town."

Lowell stepped between his brother and the doorway to the barn. "Just why did you have to go today? You were there yesterday—and the day before—and every day this week. You do have things to do around here, you know."

Ollie looked at Lowell. "I do my share of the chores." He raised his voice. "You haven't had to do anything I usually do. I make sure everything is taken care of before I go."

Lowell raised his own voice. "Sometimes things come up, and I need help, and you aren't here."

Ollie stared at him until Lowell moved from the doorway. Then Ollie led his horse inside. Lowell followed his brother into the cool interior shadows and stood watching as he unsaddled the animal and rubbed him down. For a long time, neither of them said anything.

Finally, Lowell walked over to the stall and leaned one elbow on the half wall. "I suppose you saw Rissa again." It was a statement, not a question.

Ollie stopped grooming the horse and stood silent for a minute. Then he turned toward him. "Yes, I saw her. She was visiting with Anna and Gerda. They've become friends. I think it's good for Rissa. I don't think she's ever had any women friends."

Lowell snorted as he stood up. "Maybe that's because she's just a girl." He crossed his arms over his chest.

"You haven't seen her lately, have you? I wouldn't call her a girl." Ollie resumed working on the horse. "She's a little thing, but she's all woman."

Lowell knew she was a woman. He remembered when the Le Blancs had been in Litchfield earlier in the spring. He carried a picture of her in his head, which he often allowed to take over his thoughts. Lowell wanted to touch her ebony curls. He was sure they would be soft as silk. Her lilting laugh played like a harp in his heart. Her sky blue eyes were appealing, but they looked a little shy. That part of his memory didn't agree with all Ollie had told him about Rissa now. She didn't sound as reserved as he remembered. Maybe it was time for him to see for himself.

"I'm going into town for feed," he told his brother.

He could feel Ollie's gaze boring into his back as he hitched the horses to the wagon. He didn't care. Perhaps if he saw the girl again, he wouldn't be so haunted by these thoughts.

He hadn't driven into town for awhile. Usually, he left that to Ollie, who enjoyed talking to people. Lowell liked people, but he wasn't as outgoing as his brother. When he pulled up in front of the mercantile, he glanced at the Dress Emporium. He would order the feed, then check on his sister. He loved Anna, even though she was more like Ollie. She was his baby sister and always would be. He was only one year older than she was, and she would soon be a married woman.

He tied the reins to the hitching post and turned around to come face-to-face with the woman who had filled his thoughts for so long. Standing bathed in the glow from the bright summer sunshine, she was more beautiful than he remembered.

"Hello, Miss Le Blanc."

She stared at him as if she didn't know who he was. What was wrong with her? Maybe she had forgotten meeting him. Ollie had taken up so much of her time since she'd come back to town that she might have forgotten there were two Jenson brothers.

"I know you haven't seen me for awhile. I'm Lowell Jenson." He tipped his cap.

She finally gave him a tight smile. "You're Ollie's brother, aren't you?"

Lowell nodded.

"You look a lot like him." She tilted her head and studied him from another direction. "You could almost be twins." Then she continued down the boardwalk away from him.

He entered the mercantile and browsed through the merchandise, not seeing what was in front of him. His thoughts about the young woman distracted him so much he almost forgot to order the feed. After he and Johan had loaded the gunnysacks into the wagon, Lowell went to see Anna in the dress shop.

He always felt ill at ease in the feminine place. All those female fripperies that covered every surface in the room made him nervous. He liked clean, uncluttered space. He hurried through the store to the workroom so as not to disturb anything.

Anna looked up and smiled. "Lowell, how nice to see you." She crossed the room to where he stood and gave him a hug.

He hugged her back stiffly with one arm. He never understood why she and Ollie liked all this touching, but he did love her.

"So how are you doing?" Anna took an interest in everyone around her.

"Fine." He shoved his hands into the back pockets of his jeans. It was the safest place to keep them. "I had to come for feed—for the horses."

Anna raised her brows. "Why didn't you ask Ollie to get it for you? He was here earlier."

Lowell rocked up on his toes and back down. "I know, but I hadn't been to town for awhile. I thought I might as well come."

Anna opened her mouth, but Lowell stopped her before she could ask any more questions. "I need to get back to the farm. It's time to feed the horses."

She just nodded and walked out to the wagon with him, then hugged him again.

On the ride home, he mulled over what had happened in town. He remembered Miss Le Blanc—Rissa—being more friendly to him when she was there before. Now it was almost as if she had never met him. It was Ollie's fault. He had turned her against him. It was the first time in Lowell's life he'd felt drawn to a woman, and Ollie had already messed it up. His brother could have any woman he wanted, so why did he choose the one who interested Lowell? He had been so disappointed when the Le Blancs left town the first time.

Lowell had started to think he might have a chance to establish a relationship with Rissa this time. Now he wasn't so sure.

Ollie hurried across the barnyard to help Lowell unload the sacks of feed. Neither one spoke or looked at the other as they carried the sacks into the storeroom. They just stared at the ground as they tramped back and forth. When they'd put away the last sack, Ollie started unhitching the horses.

"You don't have to do that. I can take care of it." Lowell didn't want his brother to do him any favors.

Ollie stared at him, then turned back to the horses. "It's okay. I don't want you saying I don't do my share around here."

Lowell put his hands on his hips. "You've done enough as it is." He knew it sounded harsh, but he didn't care. He had worked himself into a frenzy over that woman.

Ollie stopped what he was doing and turned to face him. "Just what do you mean by that?"

Lowell glared at him. "As if you didn't know." He turned to walk off.

His brother grabbed him by the shoulder and jerked him around.

It was too bad he was now as big and strong as Lowell. "Why did you do that?"

"I want to know what you're talking about."

"You've turned that girl against me," Lowell blurted out.

Ollie's mouth dropped open, and he shook his head. "I don't know what you mean. I haven't done anything."

Anger clouded Lowell's thoughts, raising the timbre of his voice as his temper grew. "Then why didn't she seem to know me when I was in town?"

"You went to town to see Rissa?" Ollie almost choked on the shouted question. "I can't believe this! Why would you do that? You knew I was spending time with her!"

They stood toe-to-toe, glaring at each other with fists clenched. Lowell never would hit his brother, but if he hit first—

"Boys, I want to have a word with the two of you."

The sound of their father's voice was like a bucket of cold water, splashing against the anger they both felt. They turned and saw him standing in the doorway to the barn. "Let's go inside and sit down."

They followed their father into the shadowy dimness of the building and sat on two bales of hay. The older man towered over his sons.

"I don't like what I've been seeing and hearing lately." He looked at Lowell, then at Ollie. "I don't know what has gotten into the two of you, but we can't run a successful horse farm if you're bickering all the time. It's not the way brothers should treat each other."

Lowell stood and turned away. He wondered how much his father had heard. Probably a lot since they were so loud. He didn't like his father treating him as if he were still a child.

He turned back around. "We'll take care of it, Father." He glared at his brother. "Won't we?"

Ollie glanced from Lowell to his father and back.

Their father looked at each brother in turn. "Just see that you do."

❧

It had been two weeks since they had come to Litchfield. Clarissa had enjoyed every minute of the time. Now she would have to leave, and she didn't want to. Pierre told her after breakfast to be ready to depart by nine o'clock this morning. So here she was in the parlor waiting for him to come with the surrey.

"There you are, Rissa, dear." Mrs. Olson bustled into the

room with a picnic basket over her arm. "Your father asked me to fix up this food for you to take on your outing today. He said you might be gone until after dinner tonight. Where are you going?"

Clarissa turned from watching out the front windows. "He wants me to see as much of the beautiful Minnesota landscape as possible while we're here. We'll probably take several trips to explore before we leave."

"You be careful," Mrs. Olson said. "It may be 1895, but some parts of our state are still pretty wild. Don't stray too far off the beaten path."

Clarissa laughed. "I am sure we won't go anywhere dangerous."

The sound of horses and the wagon pulled her attention back to the window. She took the heavy basket from their landlady and again thanked her before stepping out onto the front porch.

"There you are, Rissa." Pierre came up the walk and relieved her of her burden. "The sooner we get on the road, the more we can see." He stowed the basket in the back, then helped Clarissa onto the seat. He clicked his tongue at the horses, and they started toward the main thoroughfare from town. When they had ridden completely out of sight, Pierre turned the wagon onto an overgrown trail.

"Why didn't you bring the surrey?" Clarissa asked. "It's so much more comfortable to ride in."

"As you know, we'll have to cross a lot of rough terrain to reach the campsite. It wouldn't be good for the surrey. This wagon is fine." Pierre's eyes gleamed. "What's the matter, Rissa? Don't you want to leave the comforts of town?"

She glared at him, crossed her arms, and turned away. The wagon hit a deep rut, and she almost fell out. She grabbed the edge of the seat and clung to it while Pierre's laughter pealed across the rolling plains.

No, she didn't want to leave the comforts of town or anything else that was there, especially Ollie Jenson. She wouldn't see him again for two weeks, and a lot could happen in two weeks. How she hated this life! She was glad Pierre had left her in town when he returned to the campsite a week ago. She'd hoped he would do it again, but he hadn't. They rode for over an hour in silence. The sun moved higher in the sky, and Clarissa unfurled her ruffled parasol and held it over her head to protect her face from the damaging rays.

"You're not very talkative today, Rissa." Pierre finally broke the silence. "You're not pouting, are you?" She glared at him again. "It won't do you any good, and it puts the most unbecoming wrinkles on those creamy smooth cheeks."

He raised his hand as if he might touch her face, and she quickly turned away. She hated it when he touched her, and he knew it. She thought he did it just to torment her.

After crossing the grassy prairie, they entered an area of rolling hills dotted with rocks and scrub brush. Traveling deeper into the hills, they came to trees with thick undergrowth. Pierre had to concentrate on his driving there, and Clarissa was glad. It kept his attention away from her. She began to wonder what they would find when they reached the campsite. At least the overhanging branches protected her from the sunlight, so she was able to put her parasol away.

She enjoyed listening to the sounds in the woods. Birds flitted through the top branches, calling to each other in a melodious cacophony. Sometimes she caught sight of colorful plumage. Besides the usual browns she saw an occasional flash of yellow, red, or blue. Clarissa wished she were as free as those birds. She was sure small animals lived among the underbrush. She could hear scrambling interspersed with the sound of the horses' hooves clopping on the rocky soil.

Finally, they pulled into a large clearing hidden deep inside the tangle of tall trees and thick underbrush. Clarissa wondered how Pierre had found it in the first place, but he had always managed to find a similar campsite, no matter what state they were in.

A young woman, dressed in trousers and a man's shirt, hopped out of the caravan wagon that sat under a small grove of trees near the center of the clearing. She gave a vigorous wave and started running toward the wagon. Her long ebony curls were unfettered, so they flew out behind her like a flag fluttering in the wind.

"Clari!" she shouted.

After all his years in the family, Pierre understood how close the sisters were, so he stopped the wagon and let Clarissa clamber over the wheel. She ran toward her sister with her arms outstretched. "Mari!"

It felt so good to hold Mari in her arms again. Clarissa had never liked being separated from her twin, but about the only time they spent together was traveling from one place to another in the caravan. As soon as they reached a destination, Pierre would set up the confidence game so they were never seen at the same time. Their few hours together before they switched places had to suffice. But it never did. Of course, occasionally Pierre had to scout a new location. Then he would take the girls to an out-of-the-way place, and they stayed together for a few days. Precious days that were too few.

When the sisters finally quit dancing around and hugging each other, Clarissa walked with Marissa back to the campsite. Pierre had passed them and driven the wagon under the trees. He unhitched the horses and hobbled them in a grassy spot close enough to the small lake where they could graze and drink their fill. He pulled the basket Mrs. Olson had fixed for them from the back of the wagon and opened it. Soon they were enjoying fried chicken, homemade bread, fresh vegetables, and apple crumb cake. Mrs. Olson had even put homemade pickles in the basket. It was a wonderful feast.

"This is delicious." Marissa wiped her mouth on a napkin. "Do you eat like this all the time, Clari?"

Clarissa nodded. "Mrs. Olson is a very good cook."

Marissa smiled at her. "Don't eat too much, or our clothes won't fit you."

The sisters laughed.

Pierre didn't join them. "I watch to see she doesn't. It's too important."

His comments put a damper on the festive feeling the young women had been sharing. The real reason they were apart always did that.

"Pierre." Marissa was usually the one who didn't complain. "Please, please let us stop. Don't we have enough money yet?"

His glare could have turned fresh milk to clabber. "Don't start."

"But you know how much we hate what we're doing," Clarissa agreed with her sister. "Why do we have to continue?"

Pierre started packing the things back into the basket. "If this is the thanks I get for bringing you fresh food—"

"I'm sorry, Pierre." Marissa was almost crying. "I really do appreciate it. Don't take it away."

He looked from one girl to the other. "Don't worry. You'll be eating well for awhile. You're going back to town with me. It's Clarissa who won't have the food."

He stared at her. She knew he wanted an apology, but it stuck in her throat. Then she remembered she would have only smoked meat, canned beans and peaches, biscuits, and whatever she could scrounge from the woods. "I'm sorry, Pierre. Please don't take the food away."

He laughed such an evil laugh that it sliced into Clarissa's spirit. How could they fight him? He always told them they were as guilty as he was and would go to jail if he did. Would being in prison be any worse than how they lived now? She often wondered.

After lunch, Pierre unloaded other things from the wagon. He had rented it the day before and gone into a neighboring town to buy supplies, which he'd hidden under a tarp.

"Look, Clarissa—I bought some eggs and bacon. They'll last a few days if you store them in that cool spring that feeds the lake."

"Thank you, Pierre." Clarissa almost choked on the words, but she knew if she didn't say them he would retaliate, maybe even against Mari. That hurt more than when he did something to her. Her sister wasn't as strong as she was.

While Pierre lay under a tree and dozed, the sisters explored the area together. Mari showed her some wild gooseberries. In the last few days, she had picked some and used them to make desserts for herself; but more would ripen for the next week or two so Clarissa could enjoy them too. Mari also took her upstream to a waterfall with an indentation in the rock behind it. She said she used it to bathe and wash her hair. Clarissa knew she would enjoy that too. This was much better than most of their campsites had been.

Just as they returned to camp, Pierre sat up and stretched. "It's about time to start back, so get ready."

The girls went into the caravan and switched clothing. While they were changing, Clarissa told her sister about the four dresses Pierre had ordered from the Dress Emporium.

She had already taken one to her room in the boardinghouse, but the other three weren't started yet. The Dress Emporium was busy, and Pierre had told Anna and Gerda there was no hurry for the dresses.

Clarissa also told Mari how she had become good friends with Anna and Gerda and Anna's brother. She tried to make the transition as easy on her sister as she could, but it was always harder for Mari than it was for her.

Before Mari got into the wagon to drive off with Pierre, Clarissa hugged her. It was hard to let go, knowing that for the next two or more weeks the only person she would see was Pierre when he came to bring her more provisions. It wasn't as hard on Mari when she was the one to stay at the camp. She was quieter, but Clarissa liked to have people around her. It would be lonely.

Clarissa watched them drive away until the shadows swallowed up the wagon in the forest. Then she went into the caravan, threw herself on the bed, and cried herself to sleep.

four

Marissa twisted around on the wagon seat so she could see her sister as long as possible. Every time they were separated, she felt as if her heart were torn apart. They were two different and distinct personalities, but Marissa felt as if Clari were her other half—the brighter, smarter half. Marissa longed for the days before Pierre married their mother. She and Clari had been together constantly. During the early days of the marriage, he started separating them as much as he could. He told Mother their close relationship was unhealthy, and they would never develop into the women they should if they didn't do more things apart.

Unfortunately, Mother agreed with him. Clari adapted well with the new activities, but Marissa had never adjusted. While Clari became more outgoing, Marissa withdrew into herself. That was why this confidence game they were pulling was so painful. Every time it happened, something died inside her. She felt guilty, dirty, and unredeemable. Of course, it didn't help when Pierre told her she was as guilty as he was. It reinforced what she already felt.

"You can turn around now," Pierre sneered. "You won't see her for two weeks." Then he laughed. An evil laugh that echoed through the thick forest and bounced back to haunt her.

Marissa turned toward the front of the wagon and straightened her shoulders. She wouldn't let him know how much he hurt her. If she did, he'd only chide her more harshly.

Marissa didn't like this journey through the forest. It was

too shadowy. It reminded her of one of the enchanted forests in the fairy tales Mother had read to them. Any moment, she expected an ogre to step out from behind a tree and attack, or at least growl. She enjoyed life in the pleasant glade, but now she was back in the evil forest. Even the sound of birds singing had quieted with the coming of twilight—twilight that made the forest shadows darken. Would they never get through this horrible place?

Though much of the journey to Litchfield took them over uneven ground, Marissa didn't mind it. They were out in the open, away from the shadows that mirrored the darkness deep inside her.

When they reached town, the streets were silent—all except the one where the saloon was located. At least they didn't drive down that one. Near the train depot, Pierre turned the wagon across the tracks and into a quiet residential area. When he pulled up in front of a lovely two-story Victorian house, Marissa studied it with interest. The pleasant aroma of the evening meal wafted on the air, causing her stomach to give an unladylike growl. Before Pierre could help her down, she climbed over the wheel of the wagon. She didn't like his touching her. Clari had told her she didn't either, but both of the sisters had noticed he took every opportunity to do so.

"Mr. Le Blanc, Rissa, I was afraid you weren't going to make it back before dinner was over." Marissa looked up at the motherly woman who had come out on the front porch. "All the other boarders are eating now. Come on in. I set places for you, just in case."

Marissa followed her through the door into the front hall. She was glad they weren't staying at the hotel. Living in this house, she could pretend she was like most people.

"Rissa, dear, did you enjoy the sightseeing?"

Marissa looked into the woman's kind face and smiled. "Yes, the day was very interesting."

That seemed to satisfy the woman's curiosity. She led Marissa into the dining room. All conversations around the large table ceased as everyone looked at Marissa. She wanted to sink into the floor, but she stiffened her backbone and smiled. She saw at least one person she knew. August. *Let's see—what was his last name? Nilsson, wasn't it?*

The big blacksmith stood and pulled out the chair next to him. Marissa sat in the proffered seat and gave him a shy smile.

When Marissa was finally alone in the room she and Clari shared, she sank onto the chair and wilted. The evening meal had been difficult for her. She had to pretend she knew all those people. Clari had told her about them, but the information was sketchy. This room was heavenly, though. A real room in a real house. For a moment, she felt like a regular person. Then reality set in. She actually enjoyed the time at the campsite. She could relax and be herself there. Here she would have to be alert all the time, playing a role. The role of Rissa Le Blanc, a fictional person who didn't have anything in common with Marissa Voss. She sighed and hung her head.

She allowed a few moments to feel sorry for herself, then she resolved to make the most of this wonderful room while she had it. She walked over to the bed and pressed both hands on it to test the mattress. Clari had said it was soft. Marissa hadn't imagined how soft. She crossed to the high-boy and opened the drawers, one at a time, to familiarize herself with where each thing was stored. After reopening the third drawer, she extracted a nightgown and dressed for bed. By the time she nestled into the welcoming cocoon, she had pushed her negative thoughts into a hidden recess of her mind. She could play this part as well as Clari did. Their very lives depended on it.

⋅⋅⋅

When Marissa walked through the door of the Dress Emporium the next morning, Anna and Gerda weren't in the showroom. They must be working in the back. It gave her time to refamiliarize herself with the shop. Lots of new accessories were cleverly displayed on various pieces of furniture. She walked around the shop and fingered several delicate, handmade lace items. Olina Nilsson must have been busy to create all these lovely things. Even the shawl Pierre had purchased before had been replaced, but the new one was white instead of blue. She might ask him if she could have that one too. He didn't often turn down anything she asked for when other people were around. He wanted to appear wealthy and generous. But, as the girls played a part, he was playing his.

The curtains that separated the shop from the workroom parted, and Anna came through the opening. "I thought I heard the bell." She smiled at Marissa. "Rissa, I'm so glad you came by. We've finished your second dress. I want you to try it on." She led the way into the back room where Gerda sat hemming a dark skirt.

The dress they had finished for her was beautiful. Marissa went behind the screen and changed into it. When she came out and looked at herself in the cheval glass, she was pleased with what she saw. She would enjoy wearing this gown. After changing into her other clothes, she looked at the fabric Anna was spreading on the cutting table.

"Is that for one of my other dresses?" Marissa asked.

Anna nodded. "We'll try to get both of them finished before we have to start anything else. I know your father told us you weren't in a hurry, but we don't want to take too long, do we?"

Gerda agreed, and Marissa looked around the room. They had so much fabric, lace, buttons, and other notions. The variety fascinated her. She glanced again at the fabric on the table. It was a vibrant emerald green. Marissa knew she would never feel comfortable wearing that color. Why did Clari always pick such intense colors? Marissa was happier in softer shades.

"Anna"—Marissa gave her a pleading look—"would it be all right if I changed the color, since you haven't cut it out yet?"

Anna glanced at Gerda, then back at Marissa. "Are you sure? I thought you loved this shade of green."

"I do." Marissa almost choked on that lie. "But since it's summer, maybe I should wear lighter colors. Do you have a softer green?"

Anna folded up the fabric, then looked thoughtfully at Marissa, who had to turn away from the intense scrutiny. "Let's go see what's on the shelves in the shop."

Marissa was glad when she spied a bolt of light green, a softer color with a tiny white flower woven into it. She pointed toward the bolt. "I like that piece. Would it work as well?"

Anna pulled it from the shelf and spread it across the counter. "It might look better in the other style we haven't made yet."

Marissa ran her hand gently across the smooth fabric. "I would like that."

Gerda joined them in the front room. "That piece won't work as well with this pattern—"

"We're going to use it for the other style," Anna interrupted her.

Gerda looked confused. Marissa hoped she wasn't making too much trouble for the two women. She knew Clari liked them, and she hoped she would get to know them better.

"What about this pattern?" Gerda held up the picture of the style they had planned to use for the emerald-colored lawn material. "What fabric should we use for it?"

Marissa was drawn to a light lavender silk. "Could we use this?"

She couldn't understand why the other two women looked so stunned. What had she done now? How could she fix the problem if she didn't know what it was?

"Or, if not, maybe you could suggest some other material."

Anna spoke first. "No. That's all right. We'll use whatever you want. After all, the dress is for you." She picked up the two bolts of fabric and carried them into the workroom, leaving Gerda and Marissa alone.

Marissa walked over to the shawl that was arranged over a rocking chair. She didn't remember that piece of furniture being in the dress shop when she was here before. She picked up the garment and draped it around her shoulders. Then she walked to the mirror and studied how it looked on her.

She turned back around and found Gerda watching her. "I like this. I think I'll ask Pierre to buy it for me the next time he comes with me."

When Marissa returned to the boardinghouse, she pondered what had happened at the dress shop. Almost every time she looked at Anna or Gerda, they had a funny expression on their faces. It made her feel odd. Did they know who she was and what she was doing? Was that why they kept looking at her that way?

When she was alone at the campsite, Marissa enjoyed reading novels. Pierre was glad to supply plenty of them. One of her favorites was *The Scarlet Letter* by Nathaniel Hawthorne. Now she felt as if she wore a sign as Hester did in the book. How fitting her dress was in red, which was not a color Marissa liked to wear. Only hers wasn't a letter *A* for adultery. Would it be a *C* for criminal or an *L* for liar?

She threw herself across the bed. "Mother, why did you have to die and leave us in the hands of that man?" Her crying tired her out. She slept the rest of the day and through the night on top of the covers of her bed.

❧

One of the horses had thrown a shoe. Ollie almost wanted to send Lowell to town instead, since he so often complained about Ollie not doing his share of the work. But this was work. And Ollie wasn't going to let him change what he did. He was an adult, and he wasn't doing anything wrong.

The closer he got to town, the more his thoughts turned to Rissa. It would take a little while for August to shoe the horse. He might have to wait in line, so he should have time to go to the dress shop. If Rissa wasn't there, he'd check the mercantile and the ice cream shop. He knew she liked ice cream.

At the blacksmith shop, August was waiting on a stranger. Ollie tied the horse he'd led into town to the hitching post in front of the shop. He told August he'd return in about an hour to check on the work. That should give August time to finish what he was doing.

He rode his own horse to the dress shop, then hitched him in front of the mercantile. He glanced up and down the street. Rissa was just coming out of the ice cream shop. He leaned his arms on the saddle and watched her cross the street, heading for the Dress Emporium. He couldn't ask her to get an ice cream with him, but he could go in and visit with her. She didn't look up before she pushed the door open. That was strange. He never before had seen her walk with her eyes studying the boards in the sidewalk. He hoped nothing was wrong with her.

He opened the door, and the shop bell tinkled. Rissa glanced back toward the entrance. Her gaze encountered his. She blushed and looked at the floor, then turned and hurried into the workroom.

Ollie followed her through the curtains. Both Anna and Gerda looked up when his boots sounded on the wooden floor.

"Ollie!" Anna jumped up and came over to hug him. "It's good to see you. You haven't been coming to town as often as you did." She turned a puzzled look at Rissa, who was studying a folded dress lying on one of the shelves.

He thought it odd that Rissa hadn't greeted him warmly. He'd come to town in hopes of basking in her sunny smile, but something must be wrong.

Before he had a chance to ask her if she wasn't feeling well, she scooted through the curtains. "I'll come back when you're not busy," she said softly to Anna.

The bell on the front door tinkled.

Ollie furrowed his brows. "Is something wrong with Rissa?"

Anna and Gerda glanced at each other.

"Is anyone going to tell me what's going on?" He didn't care if he did sound frustrated. He was.

❧

Lowell saw Ollie as soon as he returned to the farm. "Did you just get back from town again?"

"Now don't start in on me." Ollie frowned. "I had to take the palomino. She threw a shoe."

Lowell stepped back. "Okay." He hesitated a moment. "Did something bad happen while you were in town? You weren't in this kind of mood before you left, were you?"

Ollie stopped and took a deep breath, then looked at Lowell. "Something funny is going on, and I don't understand it."

"So what seems to be the problem?"

Ollie kept staring at Lowell. Finally, he took off his cap and tapped it against his leg. "I don't understand that woman."

Lowell didn't have to ask what woman. He knew it was Rissa. What had she done now?

It had been a dry summer. The wind blew a little whirlwind of dust around their booted feet. Ollie kicked at the small dust funnel as if it were a living thing.

"It was almost as if she didn't know me. She hurried out of the dress shop right after I got there." He rubbed the back of his neck with his other hand. "When I asked Anna and Gerda if Rissa was okay, they told me she had been acting strange for a couple of days. She even changed the color of fabric for two of the dresses they're making for her."

Lowell slipped his hands into the back pockets of his jeans. He could think better in that position. "Isn't that just something women do? Change their minds? Remember all the times Anna has changed hers without any reason."

Ollie turned to walk away when Lowell heard him mutter, "But she didn't even smile at me."

Lowell pitched clean hay into the stalls he'd mucked out while he mulled over what Ollie had told him. He decided he would see for himself what was going on. Without telling anyone, he saddled his horse and set out across the fields. He could get to town faster that way instead of on the road. He turned his horse down the street toward the mercantile and saw Rissa enter the front door of the Dress Emporium. Good. He would go there first.

When the bell over the door tinkled, Rissa turned from where she was talking to Anna at the counter. Their gazes met, and hers went straight to his heart. She looked so vulnerable. Some pain was hidden in the depths. He wanted to take her in his arms and tell her everything would be fine, but he didn't have the right. He wished he did.

"Lowell!" Anna crossed the room and gave him one of her exuberant hugs. "I'm glad to see you again." She linked her arm with his and pulled him toward the back of the store.

Rissa continued to gaze at him, but she had shuttered the pain, only allowing him to see her sweet smile. Nothing seemed to be wrong with her, except that now she recognized him. Not like the last time he was in town. The smile she gave him was reminiscent of the ones she had bestowed on him when the Le Blancs came to Litchfield earlier in the spring.

※

Marissa was glad to see Lowell Jenson enter the shop. Ollie's presence seemed to overwhelm her. Somehow Lowell made her feel at ease. He was restful. She wished she could stay in Litchfield forever. Maybe get to know Lowell better. Perhaps then she could lead a normal life—with a home and family. She would have to stop thinking about it, though. He wouldn't even look at her if he could see her scarlet letter. If he knew the truth about who she was and what she'd done. She'd tried to push all that into a quiet place in the back of her mind. Lowell's presence brought it to the forefront. She felt imprisoned by circumstances. Circumstances and an evil man. An evil man named Pierre Le Blanc.

five

On the way to the farm, Lowell took off his cap and stuffed it in his back pocket. He liked to feel the wind blow through his hair. It made him feel much cooler on a hot summer day. His thoughts were filled with Rissa Le Blanc. When he saw her in town, her glistening black curls were tied away from her face with a ribbon the same color as her blue eyes. It made her look more approachable than when she wore an elaborate hairstyle. She was more beautiful than he remembered, but the pain he glimpsed deep in her eyes disturbed him. What could have put it there? Had someone treated her badly, or was it something else? It made Lowell wonder about her father. No matter how many times they met, Lowell had never felt any warmth from the man. Surely he wouldn't abuse his own daughter. But something or someone had hurt her.

After he considered the things Anna and Gerda had told him when he was in town, he had to agree that Rissa was acting strangely. It wasn't any one thing she did that would cause concern; but when they were added together, it was almost as if she were a different person than the young woman he had seen a couple of weeks ago. He had heard about people who put on one face for some and another for others. People like that couldn't be trusted. But he couldn't believe Rissa was like that.

Something in his heart wanted to know her better—to help her. But how could he?

When Lowell arrived at the farm, he searched for Ollie.

He and his brother needed to talk. They had to heal the breach between them. It was important to their parents—and to both of them too. Lowell had noticed their father had not seemed as strong as he used to be. Maybe he and Ollie could take more of the responsibility for the harder work from him. Father wasn't a young man anymore.

Finally, Lowell found his brother training one of the colts with a bridle. As Ollie led the young horse around the pasture, he talked to him and rubbed his neck in a soothing manner. Lowell leaned his arms on the top rail of the wooden fence and hiked one of his booted feet onto the lower rail. He took his cap from his pocket and put it on to shade his eyes from the bright sun. Ollie was good with the young animals, that was for sure.

His brother looked up; then he led the horse over to the fence and tied the lead line to the top rail. "Did you want to see me?"

Lowell gazed at his brother. He loved him, in his own way, even if Ollie did make him angry sometimes. Maybe they could work this out. "I've been thinking about what *Fader* said earlier."

Ollie crossed his arms over his chest and stared at him. "And—?"

Lowell moved away from the fence and stuffed his hands in his back pockets. "And I think he's right."

Ollie stared hard at him but didn't say anything. Why was it so hard for Lowell to get his brother to talk to him? He talked to everyone else. After untying the lead line, Ollie started toward the stable with the young horse. Lowell followed him into the cool darkness of the barn. He sat on a bale of hay and watched Ollie carefully remove the bridle from the animal before he opened the door that led to the pasture. The colt walked through the doorway, then ran toward his mother.

Lowell leaned both forearms on his thighs and let his hands dangle between his knees. "Are you going to talk to me about this or not?"

"What do you think we can do?" At least Ollie must have been thinking about it too.

"Well, do you like the way things are going?" Lowell looked up at him.

"No, but we don't seem to agree on much right now."

Lowell stood up from the bale of hay and thrust his fingers through his windblown hair before stuffing his hands into his back pockets. "You mean, we don't agree about Rissa Le Blanc."

Ollie nodded. "That's all we don't see eye-to-eye on, isn't it?"

A headache was starting at the back of Lowell's neck. He rubbed the spot, but it didn't help. "I guess I shouldn't tell you that when I was in town earlier Rissa was more friendly than the last time I was there—but that's what happened."

Lowell kept looking down at the ground, then finally glanced up at his brother. Ollie's green eyes were like ice and bored into Lowell's.

"I don't understand that woman at all." Ollie stomped across the barn and picked up a pitchfork. He started toward the bale where his brother had been sitting only a few moments before.

Lowell didn't want to be in the way when Ollie started wielding that tool. He stepped closer to the door. "I hate for this to come between us." Silence fell over the room. Even the sound of the pitchfork slicing through the hay had ceased. "And I hate to upset *Fader*. Maybe we could just not talk about her—and maybe we could act friendly when we're working together." At the door, he turned and studied his brother.

Ollie was still holding the pitchfork. "We could try that."

Lowell nodded and walked out into the hot sunshine. Why couldn't the two of them agree? Were they so different? Maybe it was because they were adults now and their ideas weren't the same. Somehow they had to protect their father's health. He hadn't even mentioned that fact to his brother.

His ride and the talk with Ollie had made Lowell thirsty. A cold glass of water pumped straight from the well would taste good right now, so he headed up to the house. When he rounded the end of the porch, he saw his father sitting on the top step with his head drooping against his chest. He looked as if he would have fallen if he hadn't been leaning against the post. Lowell hurried toward him.

"Fader!" Lowell couldn't recall his father ever stopping work before lunch and taking a rest. "Are you all right?"

His father didn't look up when Lowell sat on the step beside him. Lowell was trying to decide what to do when his mother rushed out the front door.

"What's the shouting about?" Then she saw her husband. She dried her hands on her apron, then dropped to her knees on the floor beside him and put her hand on his shoulder. "He's burning up. I can feel it through his shirt."

Father didn't look at her, either. She threw her arms around him and pulled him back against her with his head cradled against her chest. "Lowell, he's terribly sick. Go to town and bring Dr. Bradley as fast as you can."

Lowell stood and looked down at them. "Let me help you get him up to bed first."

Mother clutched Father more tightly. "No! When you get your horse, send Ollie to help me." She started rocking back and forth and praying softly in Swedish. If he didn't already know how upset she was, that would have told him. Mother hardly ever spoke Swedish anymore.

Lowell raced to the barn. Ollie was hanging the pitchfork on its hook. He let go of the handle and turned. "Lowell, what's the matter?"

"*Fader* is very sick." Lowell saddled his horse as quickly as he could. "He's on the front porch with *Moder*. She needs your help getting him to the bedroom."

Ollie ran out the stable door just before Lowell galloped through. All the way to town, Lowell wondered what the problem could be. "*Gud*, please help me find Dr. Bradley. Let him be in town and not out on one of the farms!"

He was thankful God answered his prayer. The doctor was finishing sewing up a deep puncture wound in Kurt Madson's leg. Some farm families took care of things like that at home, but Ellie had always been squeamish, and she was going to have a baby. Lowell helped her get Kurt into the wagon while Dr. Bradley grabbed his bag.

Most days Doc kept his horse tied to the hitching post out front in case of an emergency. Lowell was glad they wouldn't have to wait for him to saddle the horse or hitch up a buggy. He wanted to get back to the farm before something terrible happened to his father.

On the ride, Doc shouted questions, and Lowell answered them over the sound of the horses galloping. By the time they arrived at the farmhouse, Doc knew as much as Lowell did about his father's condition.

Ollie was pacing on the front porch, watching the road from town. He met them at the hitching post. "I'll take care of your horse, Dr. Bradley. You go on up to see about *Fader*." He led the animal toward the barn. Lowell knew his brother would cool the horse down, give him a good brushing, and make sure he was fed.

Dr. Bradley had been to their home a number of times, but Lowell escorted him up the stairs to the bedroom his parents shared. Doc went through the door and shut it behind him. Lowell knew they didn't need him getting in the way, but he didn't want to go very far. So he hunkered down beside the door. He could hear parts of what was happening in the bedroom, but he didn't learn much. Fear for his father filled Lowell with dread. Bowing his head, he started to pray but soon ran out of words. He didn't know what else to say.

Often enough he had read the Scripture passage in Romans, chapter eight, about the Spirit making intercession. So while his heart grew heavier the longer the doctor took, he allowed the Spirit to pray for him, expressing to the heavenly Father his anguish about his earthly father.

It seemed like hours before Dr. Bradley opened the door. Lowell stood and studied his face. What he saw didn't give him much hope. The doctor looked as worried as Lowell felt.

"I'm not going to lie to you, Lowell." Dr. Bradley, a short, rotund man, looked up at Lowell's face. "I'm not sure what's wrong with your father, and I'm not sure I can help him."

Lowell could hear his mother's soft sobs and his father's heavy breathing coming from the bedroom. "What are we supposed to do?"

"These fevers can be severe. We often don't know what brings them on." The doctor started toward the staircase. "I gave your mother a list of things that might help."

Lowell followed him to the barn. Ollie was attacking bales of hay with the pitchfork. His brother was as worried as he was, but he didn't ask any questions. When anything bad was happening, Ollie always tried to hide from it as long as he could. He often lost himself in the mundane tasks around the farm, waiting and watching. Before the doctor mounted his horse, Lowell pulled his wallet out and removed the usual fee.

"You don't have to pay me right now." Doc put his foot in the stirrup and threw his other leg over the back of the mare. "I may not be able to help your father."

Lowell held the greenbacks up to him. "You were available to come when we needed you, and we like to stay current with our accounts."

The doctor stared hard into Lowell's face before he accepted the money and stuffed it in the pocket of his vest. When he was gone, Lowell and Ollie both sat on a bale of hay. Almost in unison, they dropped their heads into their hands.

After a short time, Ollie raised his head. "The doctor's expression was grim. How bad is it?"

Lowell stood and pushed his hands into his back pockets. "He doesn't know."

Ollie jumped up and started prowling around like a nervous barn cat. "What are we going to do?"

Lowell rocked up on the balls of his feet then dropped his heels with a thud onto the dirt floor. "I've been praying a lot."

"So have I."

"We're going to run this horse farm to the best of our abilities and help *Mor* do all Doc said to do to help *Far*."

six

"You will go because I said you will." Pierre leaned closer. His whispered words hissed across the table, which was draped in a white linen tablecloth and set with fine china.

Marissa closed her eyes and sighed. She was glad no one was sitting close to them in the large dining room of the hotel. They ate most meals at the boardinghouse, but Pierre occasionally took her to the restaurant for the evening meal. Usually the room was full, and he felt the exposure would help them with the confidence game he had planned. Except today he probably was wasting his money. In a way, Marissa was glad. Everything went his way much too often.

Tonight only two other tables were being used, and the people didn't look familiar. She thought they must be travelers spending the night at the hotel on their journey to somewhere else. None of them seemed to be aware that she and Pierre were sitting across the room from them.

"Why this sudden interest in church, Pierre?" She brought her attention back to the subject they were discussing.

He glared at Marissa. She was sure he was unhappy with her calling him by his first name, but she hated calling him Father. Marissa didn't remember much about her own father. She and Clari had been so young when he died. She knew he was tall, with black curly hair, much like theirs. He often pushed his curls back from his forehead. The gesture was familiar. When she was a young child, he seemed extremely tall to her. He gave her rides on his shoulders, and she felt as if she could almost touch the puffy clouds that floated in the sky above them. He ran through the open fields on the plantation, holding on to her feet to keep her from falling from her perch. If she got off balance, she would clutch his ears, and he would tell her to be careful not to pull them off. When he sat on a grassy knoll, she would carefully climb down and sit beside him as they studied the clouds, trying to find animals hiding in them. They would laugh together. Life had been full of happiness—and freedom.

"Haven't you noticed how important church is to the people who live here?" Pierre said sharply.

Marissa was sorry he'd interrupted her pleasant memories. "Yes, all the ones we know go to church."

"At least the important ones do. They're the people we want to impress. You're doing a good job with Gerda, Anna, and the Braxtons. I'm afraid Clarissa was getting a little too friendly with them. I was glad it was time to switch the two of you when I did. I didn't want her ruining anything." Pierre whispered the last sentence because the waitress was approaching the table with their plates of steaming food.

Little did he know Marissa also felt a growing friendship—especially with Gerda and Anna. The only friend she had ever had was her sister, but these women were drawing her out of her shyness. They really cared about her. If only she and Clari could stay here in Litchfield. If only they could live normal lives. If only they weren't pulling a confidence game. If only Pierre would let her and Clari go free. But she couldn't live on *if onlys*.

Pierre had ordered steaks for them, and they smelled delicious. They practically covered the plate, leaving little room for the green beans and mashed potatoes that crowded around the edges. Marissa didn't want to eat. All the pressures in her life were at war in her stomach, but she knew Pierre would be concerned if she didn't eat at least part of the meal, so she cut a piece of the tender meat. She followed that bite with a morsel she pinched off the hot buttered roll. It melted in her mouth. The more she ate, the hungrier she got, so soon she was enjoying the food as much as Pierre appeared to be.

Maybe it was because his attention had been drawn away from her to a striking woman who had come into the restaurant to dine alone. She was probably single. Married women didn't dine out alone. Everyone was looking at her, but Pierre's focus was different. His eyes devoured the woman while he mindlessly forked the food on his plate into his mouth. The looks he gave her made Marissa feel uneasy. She glanced around to see if anyone else noticed. She was thankful no one did.

If circumstances were different, Marissa was sure he would have tried to make contact with the woman. Marissa knew that often when Pierre left the sisters alone at a campsite he went into a different town to spend time with women. Mother would be distressed if she knew the kind of women he pursued. Many young women Marissa's age didn't know about that kind of female, but she had found out about them in some of the books she'd read. She wished Pierre would make a mistake here in Litchfield, such as trying to get friendly with the wrong kind of woman. She had heard of several down at the saloon, but she hadn't seen any. If he did that, maybe the people would recognize what kind of man he was. Maybe it would bring freedom to her and Clari. At least she could dream about such a wonderful thing happening.

இ

It had been a rough week. Lowell and Ollie did all their father's work in addition to their own chores, but that wasn't the hard part. Knowing their father was lying in bed, getting weaker every day, brought an emotional turmoil that sapped their strength. Their mother hardly left his side. It was all they could do to get her to go to sleep at night. Sometimes the only way was for one of them to sit with their father. This added activity drained them further. Lowell didn't remember being this exhausted.

When Anna found out about Father, she had come home and cooked a meal. Then every day after that, some woman from the church brought the noon meal. There was often enough to feed them dinner too. The brothers were working so hard that they weren't as hungry as usual. At least they didn't notice their hunger.

When the Saturday evening chores were finished, Lowell went to his parents' bedroom and insisted his mother get some rest.

"Are you boys going to church tomorrow?" She turned her weary eyes toward him.

Lowell shook his head, thinking that would be the end of the discussion, but he should have known better.

"And why not?" Mother sounded more like her usual self. "Church is important. Besides, our friends will want to know how Soren is doing and pray for him."

Lowell didn't want to add to his mother's distress, so he agreed to go.

"You'll take Ollie too, won't you?" she insisted.

Lowell glanced at his brother, who was leaning against the door facing. Ollie gave a slight nod, and Lowell smiled at his mother. "Of course. We'll both go."

Not only had the week been hard, but Saturday night, Father didn't sleep well. His restlessness kept everyone in the house awake, trying to ease his pain and help him. He didn't want to take the medicine Doc had left for him, so it was an almost impossible task. When Lowell and Ollie finally went to bed, they overslept. They knew that if they didn't want to be late for church, they would have to hurry to finish the chores and eat breakfast. Lowell was tempted to tell their mother they wouldn't go.

In addition to the horses that provided most of their livelihood, they also had the usual assortment of farm animals to provide food for the family. It took Lowell awhile to milk their two cows while his brother took care of the chickens and pigs. When he arrived back in the kitchen with the buckets of milk, his mother was cooking breakfast. He knew she hadn't gotten as much sleep as he had, but she was up early so he and Ollie could get to church. He didn't have the heart to tell her he wasn't going. He just hoped he could stay awake for the pastor's sermon.

They had a new pastor, who was only a little older than Lowell. Joseph Harrelson had been in Litchfield for a few months, and in that time, Lowell had gotten to know him well. His sermons were biblical and thought provoking. Lowell had grown in his walk with the Lord from listening to them. That was one reason he was so concerned about this thing that was happening between him and his brother. He knew he should talk to Pastor Harrelson about the problem, but he'd been too busy. When Father was better, he would make the time. Lowell felt as if it were stunting his spiritual growth, and he didn't want that to happen.

The singing had started before Lowell and Ollie rode their horses into the churchyard. But they weren't the only people who were late. A buggy pulled up while they were tying their horses to a hitching post. Pierre Le Blanc was driving, and Rissa sat on the seat, shading herself from the hot sun with a dainty ruffled parasol that matched her dress. Her black curls were pulled up in an elaborate style, topped by a small hat that perched like a mother bird on a carefully built nest. A thin veil draped her face, making her look more intriguing. . .mysterious. . .inviting.

Lowell swallowed hard and glanced at his brother out of the corner of his eye. Ollie was smiling at the woman. Once again, the knowledge that something had come between him and his brother pierced Lowell's heart. When he looked back at Rissa, she sent a shy smile his way. He walked over to the buggy.

"May I help you down?" He didn't care what her father or his brother thought.

Rissa held out her graceful hand, and he clasped it gently. With his other hand, he supported her arm as she stepped from the conveyance. She was such a tiny woman, as light as a feather. After both slippered feet were firmly on the ground, he reluctantly released her. She reached down to straighten her skirt.

"You look lovely this morning, Miss Le Blanc." He couldn't keep his voice from sounding husky.

She glanced up at him and blushed. "Please, call me Rissa." She lowered her eyes and brushed an invisible speck from her sky blue silk dress.

Lowell tipped his hat, and Mr. Le Blanc came around the buggy and took Rissa's arm. They headed toward the door of the church, leaving Lowell with his brother.

"What do you suppose they're doing here?" Ollie watched them until they were inside. "I've never seen them in church before, and we haven't missed a Sunday since they've been in town."

"I'm sure she has come to worship, as we all have." Lowell wished his brother wasn't so interested in her.

Ollie didn't look convinced. "Something's not quite right about her or her father. I can't imagine either of them worshipping. They're here for some other reason."

Lowell stood where he was while his brother entered the building. Ollie had to be wrong about Rissa. Lowell would slip in later, but right now he needed some time alone.

&

When Marissa and Pierre entered the church, the congregation was singing a song she had never heard before. Even though it was about the blood of Jesus, it sounded soothing instead of gruesome. Marissa had never liked to see blood—hers or anyone else's. She had even fainted a time or two when she or Clari was injured as a child. But the music and the words washed over her, warming something deep inside.

Pierre led the way down the aisle to two seats on the second pew. Marissa didn't like to be the center of attention, but she couldn't help it when Pierre was around.

" 'What can wash away my sins? Nothing but the blood of Jesus! What can make me whole again? Nothing but the blood of Jesus!' " Everyone else in the room sang with great gusto, as if they meant every word.

Mother had died when Marissa and Clari were ten, but before that, she had told them stories of children from the Bible. Marissa remembered baby Moses in a basket, little David who killed a giant with his slingshot, and baby Jesus in a manger. Could that be the same Jesus everyone was singing about? How could that baby take away your sins and make you whole? She faintly recalled a story about a Jesus who died; maybe that was the One they were singing about.

When the preacher began his sermon, Marissa listened to every word, although she didn't understand many of the things he said. Once, she glanced at Pierre, and he looked bored. She was sure he wasn't listening to the preacher.

It was hot in the room, even though the windows were all open. Marissa took out a folding fan from her reticule and unfurled it. The rhythmic movement of the fan didn't take her concentration from the sermon.

She didn't understand it all. He said you couldn't commit a sin for which Jesus wouldn't forgive you, if you asked Him. Marissa wondered what kind of sins these people could have committed. She was sure none of them had done anything as bad as the things Pierre made her and Clari do. She wished she could talk to someone about what had been going on in her life, but she couldn't. None of these people could know what she had done—or what she was going to have to do later. They wouldn't understand, and if Pierre found out, he would punish her for talking about it. Of course, he always made sure her clothes would cover any bruises.

After the service, Pierre spent a lot of time talking to various people he considered important. As a result, the two of them were among the last ones to head home. On the way back to the boardinghouse, Marissa told him she wanted to talk to him about something important. He looked at her from under hooded eyes, studying her as a snake studies its prey. And that's what she felt like—Pierre's prey.

When they finished eating with the other boarders, he led her to the surrey. They drove toward Lake Ripley. Near the lake, he pulled into a grove of trees and let the horses graze on the green grass that was growing close to the water. Because of the dry summer, most of the other grass had turned brown.

"Now, Marissa, what did you want to talk about?" Pierre scowled.

Marissa sat with her hands clasped tightly in her lap. She

took a deep breath and looked down at her hands while she talked. She didn't want to see his expression. If she did, she might not be able to continue.

"I don't want to do this anymore." For a moment, the only sound she heard was the birds fluttering from branch to branch above them. Nothing else moved in the heat.

"I know that. You and Clarissa have made your wishes known often enough." Pierre spoke in a monotone.

He removed a cheroot from the pocket of his vest and lit it. She had told him often enough that she didn't like for him to smoke around her, so he blew the smoke in her direction. He liked to torment her. She ignored it. She didn't want to be sidetracked from her purpose.

"I mean it this time." Marissa turned away and took another deep breath, then blurted out, "I want a fresh start, a new life."

Pierre gave a mirthless laugh. "And you think you can do that? Make a fresh start?"

Marissa dropped her gaze back to her hands and nodded.

"It was that church service, wasn't it?" Pierre sneered. "You believe all those fairy tales, don't you?"

He flicked his ashes over the side of the buggy, but some landed on her dress. Since they weren't on fire anymore, they did no damage. She brushed them from her skirt and ventured a glance in his direction. His eyes were gleaming.

"Do you think any of those fine people in the service today would give you a chance if they knew what you've done? Don't think such silly thoughts. You're a criminal. You have been for many years. You're as guilty as I am. That's what everyone will think if we are ever caught." He took another long draw on the awful-smelling little cigar.

Tears made their way down her cheeks. Pierre didn't care about them, but she couldn't stop.

"There is no way out of the life we lead. Even if you left me, how could you afford to live? The only thing you could do is sell your body." He knew that thought would disgust her. He always used that argument when she or Clari begged him to stop their life of crime.

A slight breeze shook the trees above them, but it wasn't what caused the chills to run up and down Marissa's spine. Pierre's words did.

"You wouldn't want to do that, would you?" His voice was quiet but harsh.

The very thought was abhorrent to her. She shook her head, and the hope that had started to take root in her heart withered.

♣

Lowell and Ollie rode back to the farm in silence, each lost in his own thoughts. Lowell had slipped into the service right before the sermon. Joseph's words went straight to his heart. He knew the Lord wouldn't like this breach between Ollie and him.

After the service, while everyone was visiting in the churchyard, many people had asked about their father. Their friends committed to pray for him and for the family. Some even offered to help with the chores, but Lowell told them everything was under control right now. During that time, he watched Rissa and her father. Le Blanc seemed to be working the crowd, much as a politician would. What did he want from these people? It had to be something.

Several times Lowell caught Rissa looking at him. She gave him a shy smile, and he returned it. Just when he decided to go over and talk to her, Ollie approached her. Lowell didn't know what he said, but she didn't smile at him. Soon Ollie moved away. Now, on the trip home, the chasm between the brothers was as wide as it had ever been. How could they overcome it?

❧

Marissa didn't feel like talking to anyone after the discussion yesterday with Pierre. So she stayed in her room. She didn't go to the Dress Emporium or the mercantile, as she usually did. The words she had heard at church still tugged at her heart. She longed for what seemed to be just out of reach.

"Rissa." A knock on her door accompanied Pierre's voice. "I need to talk to you."

She opened it reluctantly. He stepped into the room and pulled the door shut behind him. He walked to the window, then looked out while he talked to her.

"Our chance is coming up soon." He turned and smiled at her.

Those words struck fear in her heart. She didn't want the chance to come anytime, especially not soon. When it did, her life here was over.

Pierre pulled a handbill from his pocket. He thrust it toward her. An artist's rendition of a circus parade, complete with a woman riding an elephant, marched across the top of the handbill. The circus was coming to town.

"I talked to the front man for the circus. They're making Litchfield their last stop before the circus train heads for their winter quarters in Florida. After I talked to him, I checked around town." He turned and smiled. "No one here has ever seen the circus. That's good for us. Most everyone will attend out of curiosity. This town will be ripe for the picking. We should have no trouble with our plans." He rubbed his hands together and gave his evil smile. Then he stuck one hand in his pocket and jingled the coins there.

For a moment, Marissa felt brave. "I've never seen a circus, either. I want to go."

Pierre frowned. "You won't be going. Clarissa will. You are much better at the other part of the plan than she is."

With his words, the last vestiges of hope she had hidden in her heart died.

seven

Lowell hoped the doctor would be able to help his father. Every day Father suffered more and grew weaker. Dr. Bradley couldn't find what caused the terrible fever. It had to be some kind of infection, but what? Doc told Lowell he had sent telegrams to several colleagues in other states, trying to find out if anyone had seen symptoms like this. He also ordered medical books to add to his library. When he wasn't treating patients, he studied them, trying to find something that would explain this malady so he could treat it.

As Lowell worked on the farm, he prayed for his father, and he prayed for Doc to find an answer that would bring relief. Of course, a miracle would be welcome too. But most days he felt as if his prayers didn't get past the roof of the barn. If he was in the pasture, he was sure they got caught in the treetops nearby. God seemed far away. Lowell figured the problem he and Ollie were having hindered his prayers.

Of course, he and Ollie no longer exchanged cross words. They just didn't talk to each other when no one else was around. They didn't seem to have anything left to say. A tiny woman with black curly hair and sky blue eyes stood between them. Even though she was short, her presence provided a wall that neither of them could—or would—scale.

Lowell didn't like what was happening, but every time he decided to agree with Ollie about Rissa, he remembered the hurt he had glimpsed deep in her eyes. He couldn't believe she was the kind of person his brother thought she was. He didn't think she was devious or two-faced. Lowell had seen a purity within her, but something held her captive. He was beginning to believe it was her father. What kind of hold did he have on her? Lowell hoped he could help her find a way to get away from whatever was causing her such pain. He had never seen any bruises on her body, but most of it was always covered, so he couldn't be sure. If Le Blanc was beating her, Lowell would gladly show him how it felt.

❧

Ollie enjoyed spending time with the horses. They were undemanding and loved him unconditionally, not like some people in his family. While his brother did the other chores on the farm, Ollie took care of the horses. With soothing words and gentle hands, he fed them, groomed them, and slowly trained each one.

All the time he spent in the stable or pasture, his thoughts were constantly drawn toward the woman who kept him tied in knots. Only a couple of weeks ago, he'd spent every minute he could squeeze out of his busy day in town with Rissa. Her smiling eyes and quick wit drew him like a magnet. She had been interested in him. He had seen it in her eyes and heard it in the lilt of her voice. He didn't know a lot about women, but he knew that for a certainty. Now she was an iceberg—cold and unmoving. She had time to smile at Lowell, but it wasn't the same as the smiles they had shared before.

Something wasn't right. No one could change his mind about that. He couldn't help believing Pierre Le Blanc was behind the change in Rissa. Ollie was sure Le Blanc didn't approve of all the time he spent with her, so he did something that caused her to change her opinion of Ollie. But what? What lies had he told her? He wanted to rush into town and confront the man, but he knew that wasn't wise.

Sometimes he wished he could throw caution to the wind and follow his heart.

It would have helped if he could talk to Lowell about this, but any mention of Rissa raised an insurmountable barrier between the two of them. It was better not to talk about her at all. They could never agree anyway.

When they were younger, Ollie looked up to Lowell. He was the best brother a boy could have, always looking after him and teaching him things. As they grew older, they became best friends as well as brothers. That was one reason they worked so well together. In such a short period of time, all that had changed. They were like strangers, and their estrangement affected every facet of their lives, even the other members of the family.

Since it was almost lunchtime, Ollie led the colt he was working with into the stable. After seeing to the horse's needs, he headed up to the house to see if he could help get the meal on the table. Sometimes the women who brought the food served it; other times they didn't. He wanted to be sure Mother wasn't disturbed. She needed to stay with Father.

Ollie was washing his hands in the kitchen sink when he heard his mother call. "Ollie, is that you?" Somehow she always knew which son it was. They must sound different, even when they weren't talking.

He hurried up the stairs, taking two steps at a time. His mother met him in the hall outside the door to his parents' bedroom. She reached to hug him, and he gathered her into his arms, hoping to comfort her somehow.

"I'm glad you've come into the house." Her voice was muffled against his broad chest, but he didn't have any trouble understanding her. "Your father insists he must speak to his lawyer." She pulled back and looked up at Ollie's face. "I told him I would send whichever one of you came into the house first. Would you please go into town and bring Mr. Jones out here as quickly as you can?"

Ollie glanced through the partially open door and saw his father was asleep. He looked so frail, almost as though he were wasting away. "Yes. I'll go right now. I can eat when I get back."

His mother patted him on the shoulder. "You are such a good son, Ollie." Then she returned to the rocking chair next to the bed.

Ollie watched her pick up her knitting. Even though her hands flew, performing the intricate needlework, she never took her eyes from his father's still form. Her lips formed soundless words, and he knew she was praying.

❧

Lowell was eating his lunch when Ollie and another man rode up. He left his half-empty plate and went to open the front door. The two men had reached the porch. "Ollie. . .Mr. Jones?" He opened the door wider, and the lawyer immediately started up the stairs. Lowell looked at his brother with a questioning expression.

Ollie shrugged. "I'm famished." He headed toward the kitchen.

Lowell followed him. "Are you going to tell me what's going on?"

Ollie dished up some beef stew with corn bread, then answered his brother's question. "*Fader* insisted on seeing his lawyer. *Moder* asked me to get him." He turned toward the table where Lowell sat. "That's all I know."

Just after Ollie sat down, their mother came into the kitchen. She said she had taken some broth up to Father earlier, but she hadn't eaten lunch. After filling a bowl from the food in the warming oven, she joined them.

For a few minutes, the only thing they did was eat. Then Lowell put his fork down and asked, "Do you know why *Fader* wants to talk to Mr. Jones?"

She shook her head. "He didn't tell me, and he didn't want me to stay in the room." She pushed her food around the bowl with a spoon.

Lowell had noticed she didn't eat much these days. He almost wished he hadn't asked his question. He hoped it wouldn't keep her from finishing lunch.

The three of them tried to make casual conversation, but it was sporadic. They took turns glancing at the ceiling as if they could see into the bedroom above and hear what was transpiring.

When he finished lunch, Lowell went outside to split some logs for the stove. But he couldn't keep his mind on what he was doing. He was afraid the ax might slip and cut him. Besides, it was hot. When he went into the kitchen to pump a glass of cold water from the well, he saw Mother in a rocking chair in the parlor. She usually worked on needlework when she was there, but now she just sat still and stared out the window. Her hands lay idle in her lap.

Lowell stepped out on the porch and prayed for his mother and father. Just as he finished and looked up, he noticed someone galloping on a horse toward the house. Dr. Bradley leaped from his mare and quickly tied her to the hitching post. Lowell met him halfway.

"I think I've discovered what's causing the infection!" Doc rushed toward the house, and Lowell had to hurry to keep up with him. "We can't lose any time treating it, if it's not too late already!"

A thought invaded Lowell's consciousness—one he had

pushed from his mind before, not letting it near. What if it was too late? He couldn't lose his father. He just couldn't. He still needed him. So did Mother—and Ollie.

Mother must have heard the commotion, because she opened the screen door before they reached it. "Come in, Dr. Bradley. What can I do to help?"

"Bring some boiling water up to the bedroom, along with clean pieces of material for compresses."

Before he could rush up the stairs, Mr. Jones came down. He tipped his hat to Lowell's mother and left quickly.

"What was he doing here?" the doctor asked.

Lowell followed him up the stairs. "*Far* wanted to see him. He's been up there for a couple of hours."

Doc frowned, then entered the bedroom and closed the door. Lowell hurried back downstairs to carry the hot water for his mother. She opened the door for him, and he set the large pan on the bedside table.

"I hate to do this, Lowell." Doc had already rolled up his sleeves to his elbows. "But I'm going to have to ask you to let your mother and me take care of your father."

Lowell glanced around the room. He wanted to help. But when he looked at his mother, he knew it would be better for her if he didn't make a fuss.

When Lowell came back downstairs, he wanted to throw something—or hit someone. If he were younger, he might have done one of those things. Instead he went out to the front porch and sat on the top step. Ollie saw him and walked over from the barn to join him. They sat and waited. Neither of them wanted to voice the fear that had invaded their hearts. It wasn't long before the doctor came out to join them, but it seemed like an eternity.

"I'm sorry." Doc was rolling his sleeves back down and

buttoning the cuffs. "I did all I could. The infection had been in his system too long."

Ollie jumped up. "Tell me he's not de—"

When his younger brother dropped his head into his hands and sobbed, Lowell went to him. He knew why his brother couldn't finish that word. How could their father be dead? As boys, Lowell had always taken care of Ollie and tried to keep him from getting hurt. Now he couldn't stop Ollie's pain; he felt the same thing.

Lowell looked at the doctor. "What caused the fever?" Tears clogged his throat.

"I finally heard from a colleague. He works near a horse farm in Kentucky. This kind of thing has happened there. If you're not careful, you can get an especially virulent infection from horse manure. Your mother and I looked your father over, and we found a cut on his shin. I think that's where the infection entered his body. But we were unable to treat it. If only I had found this out sooner, I might have been able to help him."

Lowell could tell from the expression on Doc's face that this had hurt him almost as much as it did them.

"Boys," Doc continued, "I want you to be especially careful." He looked stern. "Don't ever go into the barn or anywhere there is horse manure if you have an untreated open cut or sore. It could be deadly." He clapped his hat on his head and walked toward his horse with his head and shoulders slumped. He mounted and headed toward town, but he didn't seem to be in a hurry. His horse walked slowly down the road.

❧

The next day passed in a blur. Lowell knew his mother, Anna, Ollie, and he had made several decisions together, but he wasn't sure what they were. Mother spent most of the time in tears. Lowell fought to keep from crying. When he looked at

Ollie, he could tell he was having the same battle. Once Doc reached town, word spread quickly. August brought Anna to the house so she could be with the family. A couple of neighbor women came and helped Mother get Father ready for the viewing. The town had an undertaker, but he was a stranger. They didn't want to take Father to him. Neighbors and church members sat with them around the clock until the funeral. Bennel, Gustaf, and August Nilsson worked together to build the casket.

After the service in church, Gustaf and August drove the wagon carrying the casket to the knoll above the Jenson house where Father wanted to be buried. He and Mother had already decided to have the family cemetery in the small grove of trees on that hill. Father's was the first.

After a brief graveside service, Lowell and Ollie decided they would build a white picket fence to enclose enough ground for the next few generations of Jensons. They also were going to order a headstone from a stonemason in St. Paul.

Now most of the neighbors had gone home, and Mother was finally resting. Lowell and Ollie sat on the front porch, drinking glasses of lemonade someone had brought to them. Soon August and Anna joined them and sat on the swing, and August put his arm around Anna.

"How are we going to get along without *Fader?*" Ollie's plaintive question reached out to Lowell.

It repeated the one that had haunted Lowell. What would they do? He didn't want to think about it today, but he couldn't ignore it for long.

"I always thought he would be here for my children." Lowell glanced at his brother. "I wanted him to teach my sons the things he taught us. He could do a much better job of it than I'll be able to."

Ollie nodded. "Life doesn't always happen the way we think it will, does it?"

Lowell leaned his head against one of the pillars holding up the roof of the porch. He closed his eyes, trying to keep the tears at bay. Men weren't supposed to cry, but he was having a hard time not doing so. According to the wet trails making their way down Ollie's cheeks, his brother shared the same problem.

After a few moments, Lowell became aware of the sound of a horse making its way toward the house. Probably another neighbor bringing food or something else for Mother. He opened his eyes and turned to look at the lone rider. Mr. Jones dismounted at the hitching post in front of the house. Lowell wasn't sure he was glad to see him. Lawyers often didn't bring good news. Surely if he had bad news, he would have waited to come another day.

Mr. Jones walked up to the porch. He took off his hat and held it in both hands as he looked at the brothers. "I'm sorry to come on such a sad day, but it was your father's instructions I should come the day he was buried."

Lowell glanced at his brother. Ollie just stared at the lawyer.

Lowell turned and did the same thing. "Our mother is resting, and this isn't a good time. Can't you come back later?"

"No." Mother's voice came through the screen door. "I'm up now, Lowell. Ask Mr. Jones in for a cool drink. I'm sure he's thirsty on such a hot, dry day."

Lowell and Ollie led the way into the parlor. August and Anna followed the lawyer. It was even hot in the house. If there had been any kind of wind, it would have blown through the open windows and cooled the room some, but there wasn't even a hint of a breeze. One of the women who was cleaning the kitchen brought a pitcher of lemonade and a glass for Mr. Jones; then she left the family alone with the lawyer. When Lowell looked at his mother, her red-rimmed eyes seemed to fill her face.

After taking a long swallow of the drink, Mr. Jones reached into the pocket of his suit jacket and removed a folded document. He cleared his throat. "This isn't my favorite thing to do, but it goes along with being a lawyer." He unfolded the pages and started reading, "I, Soren Jenson, being of sound mind. . ."

All the legal terms droned on and on. When he finished reading, Mr. Jones asked if there were any questions. Lowell was too stunned to think of any. Ollie just sat there with his hands clasped between his knees.

Mother looked at Lowell with a wan smile on her face. "Do you understand?"

"I think so." He turned toward the lawyer. "It means Ollie and I own the horse farm as equal partners. Right?"

Mr. Jones nodded.

"And we're not allowed to sell our shares for at least a year."

"Your father was specific about that provision. He mentioned there had been some. . .tension between you for awhile. By the way, that information will remain confidential between us. He hoped that by adding this provision he could help you get over this situation. By working together for a year, I mean." He cleared his throat again. Then he picked up his glass of lemonade and took another swallow.

Mother nodded. "That sounds like a good idea to me."

After Mr. Jones left, Lowell went to the barn and sat on a bale of hay. He loved this place. Surely Father knew that. He never wanted to sell it. He and Ollie were having a bit of a problem right now, but they were family. And this horse farm was their heritage. They would have worked together, even without that will. Lowell hadn't realized the situation between Ollie and him had affected the rest of the family so much. It was their own fault Father felt he had to put this in a legal document. Lowell dropped his head into his hands and sobbed.

eight

If she lived to be one hundred years old, Marissa would never understand Pierre. Of course, he was hardly ever nice to her or Clari. Since the Sunday when they attended church, he had been more brusque with her than before. She was sure it was because of their conversation later that afternoon. And he didn't take her to church again. Most days Pierre disappeared soon after breakfast. He often told her not to leave the boardinghouse because he would soon return. That was never true. Day after day she stayed in her room, reading the books he brought her. She spent a lot of time alone, and he never returned until dinnertime.

Well, today would be different. He could go away if he wanted to, but she wouldn't stay meekly in her room as he ordered. She was going to the Dress Emporium. She wanted to see Gerda and Anna. She missed talking to them.

After breakfast, he left with the usual admonishment. Marissa went upstairs and looked through her clothes, trying to decide which dress would be coolest to wear. Even though Minnesota was much farther north than any place they had been before, the month of August was hot here. If the wind wasn't blowing, she sweltered even with her windows open, and it hadn't been windy for days.

She hadn't finished dressing before Pierre knocked on her door. Why hadn't he stayed away today as he had before?

She went to the door but didn't open it. "Just a moment. I'm changing into something cooler."

"Well, hurry up." Pierre usually tried to sound nicer when they were in the boardinghouse but not today.

She fastened the buttons on the front of her bodice, then opened the door. He pushed past her and closed the door behind him.

"I'm going to take you out to the camp. You may pack one carpetbag. I told Mrs. Olson we would be gone for a few days. I want to get on the road before it gets too hot."

When he left, Marissa sat on the side of the bed, trying not to cry. She had always liked being in the campsite instead of in whatever town they were visiting. Not this time. She had made friends, and she didn't want to leave them. She wished she could stop Pierre, but he couldn't keep her from thinking what she liked. With a sigh, she stuffed several items into the carpetbag, along with some new books.

On the way to the woods, Pierre was quiet. He looked as if he had a lot on his mind. Marissa didn't want to make him mad at her, so she didn't talk, either. But she could think about anything she wanted to. She hadn't seen Lowell Jenson since the day they went to church. She wondered what it would be like if she could just be herself around him. He always paid attention to her, and his smiles reached something deep inside.

His brother, on the other hand, was sort of strange. Marissa didn't know exactly what it was about him, but she had the feeling somehow he didn't trust her. There was a very good reason not to trust her, but he couldn't know about that. So being around him made her uncomfortable.

Marissa wondered why Pierre had told Mrs. Olson they would be away a few days. She hoped that was true. Maybe he would leave her with Clari at the camp for awhile. She and Clari could relax and enjoy each other's company. She could hardly wait to talk to her sister about the Jenson brothers.

Pierre had always told Clari and her it was important to keep the camp a secret. Each time he went, he found a different way to go, to keep from making a trail someone could follow. This trip was longer than before. Pierre drove the horses faster than usual, so Marissa bounced around on the seat. She gripped the seat to keep from falling out of the wagon. At least she would see her sister soon. It had been a long time since they were able to spend more than a single day together. Marissa hoped they could be together for at least a week. And she hoped Pierre would be nowhere around, so she and Clari could relax.

When they reached the forest, Marissa closed her eyes so she wouldn't see the dark shadows; but she couldn't shut out the unidentifiable sounds that brought out her hidden fears. She was glad when the wagon entered the sunshine again. She opened her eyes and scanned the clearing, looking for some sign of Clari.

&

Clarissa was at the creek washing her clothes when she heard a wagon. She grabbed up her wet clothing and darted behind a tree. Carefully working her way toward the sound, she peeked from behind each tree before she ran to another one. Finally, she caught sight of Pierre and Mari in the wagon, which was fast approaching the campsite. She ran to the caravan and put her wet clothes on the top step. Later she could spread them on bushes to dry.

She turned and saw Pierre pull on the reins to stop the horses. "Mari!" Clarissa ran and helped her sister alight from the wagon.

"Clari!" Mari hugged her so hard she could hardly breathe. Clarissa hugged her back; then they danced around, laughing and holding each other's hands.

Pierre stood and glared at them. He knew how much they loved each other—and how much they didn't love him.

"Stop that and come help me unload the wagon."

He sounded harsher than she remembered. Either he was upset, or Clarissa had been in the camp so long she wasn't used to him anymore.

After they unloaded the supplies, Mari reached under the seat and pulled out a carpetbag. Clarissa turned a questioning face toward Pierre.

He stood in the shade of a tall tree, so his face was in shadows. "Yes, Marissa will stay with you awhile." Clarissa couldn't keep from smiling. She didn't care if it made him angry.

Mari stared at Pierre for a moment. "Pierre, please let us stop this criminal activity."

He frowned. "We've already discussed this enough, and I'm tired of your whining." He took a menacing step toward Mari.

Clarissa moved between them. "I agree with Mari. How long will you make us continue to do this?"

When Pierre laughed, it pierced Clarissa's heart. He sounded so evil. "I'm all the family you have left. I have to take care of you. Why do you question everything I do? You have nice clothes and plenty of food to eat. Most women would be happy with that."

Mari stepped up beside Clarissa. "But it's wrong, and you know it's wrong."

Pierre glared at her before he turned to Clarissa. "I made the mistake of taking Marissa to church. She has had all kinds of ideas since then."

Mari placed her fists on her hips. "I only want to live a normal life—as Gerda and Anna do." Clarissa was proud of her for taking a stand.

Pierre took Mari by the shoulders and shook her. "I told

you I didn't want you to mess anything up. You weren't supposed to make friends. That's why I brought Clarissa to the campsite earlier. She was too friendly."

Clarissa watched Mari's eyes fill with tears when Pierre grabbed her. Soon they became twin waterfalls down her cheeks. Clarissa wanted to intervene, but this had happened enough times in the past that she'd learned not to try to stop him. He wouldn't listen, and both she and her sister would be hurt far worse than Mari was today. So Clarissa clamped her teeth together and stifled her impulse to yell at him and pound him with her fists.

Mari jerked herself from his hold. "I haven't been the kind of friend to them they were to me. I want to live an honest life." She crossed her arms over her chest and thrust her chin out. Clarissa had never seen her timid sister like this.

Once again Pierre laughed. "Don't worry. We won't be here long enough for you to do that. As soon as I come back, we'll set everything in motion." He turned and sauntered toward the wagon. "I have some business to take care of getting ready for the game we'll pull in Litchfield. I don't know how long it will take, but I think it'll be about two weeks." He turned and gestured toward the large pile of items they had unloaded from the wagon. "That's why I brought so many supplies."

Marissa's eyes widened.

"You're going to leave us for two weeks?" Clarissa's voice squeaked out the last word.

Pierre nodded. "If you're careful, you'll be all right."

"What if something happens?" Marissa's voice quavered. Her bravado had been short lived.

"Nothing's going to happen." Pierre sounded disgusted. "You have a gun, and I'm going to leave one of the horses with you. If you have an emergency, you can go into town but not Litchfield." He pulled a paper from his pocket. "Here's a map that will lead you to Wayzata. You can go there in an emergency. But if I come back, and you've gone there for any other reason, you'll wish you hadn't." That last sentence was no idle threat.

Clarissa knew Mari was probably shaking in her shoes. "What about money—if we have an emergency?"

Pierre pulled a pouch from the pocket of his vest and threw it toward Clarissa. She surprised herself by catching it in midair. She was also surprised by how much the pouch weighed. He really meant he wouldn't be back for at least two weeks. Maybe he wasn't ever coming back. Maybe this was his way of getting rid of them, and this money was a payoff. Wouldn't that be wonderful?

Pierre unhitched the horses from the wagon and took them to the stream for a drink. When he returned, he hitched only one horse to the wagon. Clarissa and Mari stood and watched him in silence. They would talk after he was gone. As he drove away from them, he turned around and gave a cavalier wave just before he entered the surrounding forest.

When they could no longer see him, Mari crumpled into a heap, weeping as if her heart were broken. Clarissa sat on the ground and gathered her into her arms. She held her sister until she was cried out. Then Clarissa stood and pulled Mari up with her.

She dried Mari's eyes with her handkerchief, then stuffed it back in the pocket of her trousers. "Think about it, Mari. Pierre will be gone for two whole weeks."

❧

Marissa felt unfettered, and she knew her sister did too. Free. It was wonderful. Marissa wished it could be forever. They opened the crates and worked together to store the provisions in the caravan. Then they ran and played in the glade, as if they were still children. In the evening after eating, they sat around the campfire and talked.

"Tell me what has been happening in town," Clari inquired.

After Marissa told her about becoming friends with Anna and Gerda, Clari asked, "How is Ollie Jenson?"

"Okay, I guess." Marissa looked at Clari. "I was more interested in Lowell."

Clari laughed. "He was too quiet for me. Ollie is more fun."

Marissa understood what was going on. "You're interested in Ollie, and I'm interested in Lowell. Wouldn't it be wonderful if we could be ourselves around them?"

Clari looked thoughtful. "Oh, yes. I know it can never happen, but what if it could?" She gazed up at the clouds. "What if we were living normal lives—being ourselves—and they knew there were two of us? I wonder if they would court us the way Mother told us Father courted her."

"We wouldn't dress alike," Marissa added. "Our clothing would reflect our individual personalities. You could be Clarissa Voss, and I could be Marissa Voss, and Rissa Le Blanc would be no more."

The next morning, the sisters went to the waterfall. They stripped down to their unmentionables and romped in the pool at the base before they showered and washed their hair under the waterfall. While they let their hair dry, Marissa told Clari about the Sunday she and Pierre had attended church.

The song that had touched her heart still played through her mind. She sang as much of it as she could remember.

"I can't believe you're singing about blood." Clari sat up straighter. "You never liked it."

"I know, but something about the song soothes me. I don't know why."

"What does it mean?" Clari asked.

"I wish I knew." Marissa tried to remember what the preacher said. "In the sermon, the pastor talked about Jesus saving us from all our sins. He said we can't commit a sin Jesus won't forgive."

Clari looked confused. "I remember Mother telling us about baby Jesus in a manger, and we see things about Him at Christmas. Is this the same Jesus?"

"I think so."

"But how could that baby save us from all our sins?"

Marissa shook her head. "I don't know. I think I remember Mother telling us a little about an older Jesus too, One who died. I'd hoped Pierre would take me to church again so I could hear more of what the preacher had to say and maybe find out. I didn't even get a chance to ask Gerda and Anna about it. Pierre didn't let me go back to the Dress Emporium before he brought me out here."

⁂

When Clarissa got up the next morning, Mari was still sleeping. After leaving her sister in bed, Clarissa took a walk through the grove around the campsite. She liked early mornings. They were the only cool times of the day. She went back to the berry patch and picked some for breakfast.

The rest of the day was spent much like the first one. When evening came, the sisters cooked dinner, then sat watching the fire die down.

Mari got a dreamy expression on her face. "I've been thinking about Lowell and Ollie again. What if they did court us?"

Clarissa put her hands in the grass behind her and leaned her weight on them. "That would be wonderful!"

"It would mean we were living normal lives. Maybe we

would be in Mrs. Olson's boardinghouse, and Pierre would be gone. I wish he could be sent to prison. He deserves it." Mari drew her knees up and put her arms around her legs. "If only he could be caught, and we wouldn't. But that is impossible."

Clarissa leaned forward. "Don't start thinking bad thoughts. We need to enjoy this time together. If we lived in the boardinghouse and Lowell and Ollie were courting us, I wonder how long it would take them to ask us to marry them."

Mari leaned her chin on her knees. "Maybe they would do it at almost the same time. We could have a double wedding."

Clarissa sighed. "We've never really been to a wedding. It's silly for us to make up these stories."

"Oh, Clari, I would just die if I didn't have a little hope!"

nine

Because Ollie and Lowell were used to doing all the work around the horse farm, they had no trouble continuing after their father died. Their problems were mostly confined to their personal relationship.

They worked well together, but when they arrived back at the house in the evenings, they maintained a shaky peace at best. Every conversation led to things they disagreed about. Their differing opinions about Rissa Le Blanc affected many other things they discussed. Neither one could understand his brother's position, so discussions were short and tense. Ollie realized he was as much to blame as his brother.

The situation affected Mother too. Ollie knew it broke her heart. In addition to the grief she felt at the loss of Father, this was too much. She tried to hide how it hurt her, but Ollie recognized the signs of her pain. And he was sure his brother did too. That's why they had almost stopped talking to each other once they returned to the house after work.

One evening, Ollie asked Lowell to accompany him out to the barn when they finished dinner. He used the pretense of wanting to show him how one of the colts was progressing, but he figured Lowell had guessed he wanted to talk to him about something else. As long as he could remember, his brother had been able to read him like a book.

"Why did you ask me to come out here?" Lowell didn't lose any time getting right to the point.

His belligerent stance alerted Ollie to the fact that the

discussion might not go as he had hoped. He walked over to the closest stall and leaned his arms on the top rail, his back to his brother. It was often easier to talk to Lowell if he wasn't looking at him.

"*Moder.*"

Lowell was quiet so long Ollie finally turned to look at him.

"What about *Moder?*" Lowell asked.

"I'm sure you know how much our estrangement affects her."

Lowell nodded and rubbed the back of his neck. Then he dropped his hands to his sides. "Do you have any idea how we can overcome this? If we start talking about Rissa Le Blanc, we only argue. You think she is not what she seems, and I want to help her."

"I know." Ollie looked at the floor. He scuffed an oval in the dirt with the toe of his boot. Then he erased it. "We work together well, though."

"In the evenings, when we should be enjoying conversation, we are so careful about what we say to each other. I think about Rissa a lot. Maybe you do too. So I want to talk about her, but we're back to the problem." Lowell crossed his arms over his chest, tucking his hands under his arms. "How are we going to get past that?" He rocked up on the balls of his feet, then down again.

Ollie pushed his hands into his hip pockets, something Lowell usually did. Maybe he was more like his brother than he had thought. "How about if I let you have the house?"

"What?" Lowell looked confused. "Have the house? What are you talking about? Where would you live?"

"I've figured that out. I could build a house on another part of the property." Lowell opened his mouth, but Ollie held up his hand to stop him. "Let me finish. We'll both want to marry someday. When we do, we'll have separate homes. I don't think either one of us plans to sell his part of the horse farm. There is no reason we can't run it together."

Lowell seemed to be mulling over this information. "That's right. Do you have a spot in mind?"

"I think so. When I was out riding yesterday, I noticed it again. I was reminded that when I was younger I used to ride out there. It was my favorite spot on the farm. Tomorrow maybe we could go over there and look it over. If you agree I can use the land, I'll start building as soon as I can."

Lowell scratched his head. "I'm not sure how that would help, but it's okay with me."

Ollie looked his brother in the eyes. "Mother can live with you in the main house. It's been her home for so long. Maybe we could even eat meals together as we do now. That would make the transition of my living in another house easier on her."

Lowell didn't take his gaze from his brother's. "That should work, and she could see both of us in the evenings as she does now. Maybe it could help ease the tension too."

The only thing that will ease the tension will be for us to work out the problem about Rissa Le Blanc. Ollie knew that wouldn't happen anytime soon. His brother was interested in her— very interested. If she were the woman Ollie knew a few weeks ago, he would be interested in her too, but evidently, she had changed. That's why he didn't trust her. But his brother wouldn't hear any talk against her.

❧

When Lowell awoke the next morning, it was later than usual. He could hear the sounds of his mother in the kitchen. The aroma of bacon and biscuits that usually met him when he returned from milking the cows wafted up the stairs. It was no wonder he slept so late, because it had taken him a long time to get to sleep. His mind wouldn't let go of what he and Ollie discussed in the barn. Intermingled with those thoughts were musings about Rissa Le Blanc and pain over losing his father. He wished Father were here so he could talk to him. Maybe he could make some sense of what was happening. Lowell's thoughts had been so jumbled that he couldn't settle down. He took off his boots so he wouldn't make any noise and paced the floor of his room for hours after they all retired.

If Rissa hadn't come into their lives, he and Ollie might never have disagreed the way they did now. Thoughts of the woman warmed Lowell's heart. The memory of her soft voice and the enticing fragrance that enveloped her haunted him night and day. He wanted to get to know her better. Thoughts of having her in his life forever never left him, but Ollie's opinion of her intruded on those ideas.

Lowell hurried to don his clothes; then he took the stairs two at a time. When he arrived in the kitchen, Ollie was bringing in two buckets of warm milk. Lowell stopped short in the doorway and looked at his brother.

"You didn't have to do the milking for me."

A slow smile covered Ollie's face. "I wanted us to get an early start on our ride."

Lowell could see their friendly conversation pleased their mother. She beamed, and the twinkle had returned to her eyes.

After a hearty breakfast, the brothers set off. Since they both enjoyed a good gallop, Lowell followed Ollie's lead as they let the horses stretch their abilities to the limit. Soon Ollie slowed down. Lowell did too.

When Ollie turned his horse toward a hill, Lowell followed him. On the top of the hill, a grove of trees stood sentinel over a bluff. The small stream that flowed through the farm ran along the base of the cliff. Ollie dismounted his horse, then tied him to one of the trees. When Lowell had finished tying his horse, he went to stand beside Ollie, who was looking out over the valley surrounding the stream. The vista was beautiful and familiar. A small lake on the near horizon glistened in the bright sunshine. Since it was morning, birds flitted from branch to branch above them, and a gentle breeze whispered through the trees, cooling both the men and the horses. This site was the perfect place to build a house. The trees would serve as a windbreak in the storms of winter. Because the hill was the highest spot around, no one could sneak up on it. It was thirty years since the war, and the country was tamer now, but outlaws occasionally still roamed outlying areas.

"I think you've chosen wisely." Lowell turned toward Ollie. "I hope a house here will make you happy."

Ollie looked surprised. "You really mean that, don't you?"

Lowell nodded and threw his arm across Ollie's shoulder as they walked back to where the horses were waiting.

That evening, Ollie completed drawing plans for the house he had already been working on. He tried not to think about Rissa, but he could picture her in each of the rooms. He knew he needed to forget the woman. She was bad news for him and his brother. No woman who changed that much in only a couple of weeks would be a good wife, but he couldn't help wondering what life with her would be like—if she were the woman he remembered.

Ollie planned to build a two-story house. It would be almost as large as the main house because he wanted several children. He needed plenty of room for the family God would give him and his wife. He could imagine Rissa descending the stairs toward him with an eager smile lighting her blue eyes. He would hold out his arms, and she would slip into his embrace, her dark curls tumbling over his arms. Ollie stopped staring into space and shook his head. He had to stop this nonsense.

The next day, Ollie made a trip into town to order materials for the house. When he was finished, he sauntered into the Dress Emporium to see Anna.

After they had visited for a few minutes, Anna asked, "Have you heard about the Le Blancs?"

Ollie shook his head. "What about them?"

"August said Mrs. Olson told them Pierre and his daughter were out of town for a few days, but they said they were coming back in a week or two."

Ollie wished he didn't care, but he was glad he might see Rissa again soon. He hoped she would once more be his lively companion, for a while anyway.

Because he had telegraphed the order, the supplies arrived by train a couple of days later. About fifty men from the church—including Johan Braxton as well as August, Gustaf, and Bennel Nilsson—came to help build the outside walls and put the roof on. They put in most of the studs on both the lower floor and the upper story in a few days. Ollie wanted to finish out the inside of the house by himself. He could come over most evenings after dinner. While it was still summer, he would have enough light to work several hours. It was a good way to relieve his frustrations.

❧

Lowell worked hard to finish the chores. He even repaired some of the tack they had let go for awhile.

Ollie returned from town, and Lowell stepped out of the barn to meet him. "I want to ask you something."

Ollie dismounted and led his horse into the stable. Lowell followed him.

"Ask away, Brother." Ollie started to remove his horse's saddle.

Lowell leaned against the tack room doorframe. "I want to go on a hunting trip—if that's all right with you."

Ollie turned around, still holding the saddle. "Why wouldn't it be all right with me?"

"Well, you would have to do all the chores, and you want to work on your house."

Ollie glanced around. "It looks as if you have things under control, so it won't be too much more work." He took the saddle into the tack room and put it up. "How long will you be gone?"

Lowell moved away from the doorframe. "I don't know. I have a lot to think about. You know I like to be alone to work things out in my mind."

The next morning long before dawn, Lowell loaded a pack animal with the provisions he would need on a hunt. Besides food, he packed ammunition for his rifle and a tarp in case it rained. It had been a dry summer, but one never knew when a summer storm would blow across the plains. At least he wouldn't need a tent. It was warm enough to sleep under the stars. Lowell always enjoyed lying on his back, looking up at the indigo canopy filled with tiny lights that winked and glowed above him. When he did, he felt closer to God than at any other time. A God who could create that vast expanse had to be powerful enough to help him with any difficulty. He hoped that by the time he came home, God would help him overcome his problems.

After the provisions were loaded, he saddled his horse. He walked the two horses slowly by the house, because he didn't want to wake either his mother or Ollie. When he was far enough away that the sound wouldn't disturb them, he mounted his horse and headed toward the northwest. It had been a long time since he had ventured in that direction.

Because the land had a wilder, untamed feel to it, he usually hunted in other places. But today he wanted to get as far from civilization as he could. He just hoped he wouldn't encounter a gang of outlaws.

Lowell rode across the plains until he came to an area that was pocked with canyons and gullies. The sun was coming up, and he stopped to eat some cold biscuits and bacon his mother had cooked for him last night when he told her he was going hunting. He stopped beside a small, clear stream that tumbled over rocks. He dipped up some of the cold water with a tin cup. If he had wanted to take the time, coffee would have tasted good with the biscuits, but he was in a hurry to move farther into the wilderness.

After watering his horse, Lowell mounted and started down a gully. He was surprised to see signs of recent wagon tracks. They were faint because of the rocky soil, but here and there a distinct impression caused by the rim of a wagon wheel led deeper into the gully. Slowly, he followed the trail. Sometimes it disappeared altogether when solid rock lined the gully. Eventually, he would pick up the trail again farther on. He had never heard of anyone taking a wagon into this country. Usually travelers kept to the south where the undulating plains were easier to traverse. He wondered if a new band of outlaws he hadn't heard about yet was operating there. He would be careful—just in case.

Lowell followed the trail deeper and deeper into the wilderness where scrub brush grew from tiny patches of soil that clung to the rocks. He entered a valley surrounded by cliffs. The floor of the valley contained a dense forest. One time, when he was about twelve years old, his father had brought Ollie and him here. Lowell remembered a clearing in the forest where scattered clumps of trees created shelter good for camping. They had spent several days exploring the area. A stream entered the valley from the north ridge of the canyon and tumbled over rock formations until a waterfall, about fifteen feet tall, emptied into a pool of clear water. He and his brother had played in that pool when they got hot.

After that summer, Father didn't take them on any camping trips so far from home. He had decided to start raising horses, and all three of them worked too hard to be gone so long.

Lowell made his way through the thick trees that surrounded the valley. The dense undergrowth would be a good hiding place for bandits. He hoped he wasn't making a mistake coming here. If he could find the waterfall, he wanted to camp near it if it was safe. The tranquility of the glade might help him sort out his thoughts. Maybe God would even give him a solution to the dilemma.

Before Lowell reached the clearing, he heard faint voices. Someone was in the valley. He almost turned back, but what if it wasn't outlaws? What if someone else had found this place of refuge? The valley was large. It would be easy to camp out of sight from the others. They didn't have to have any contact, but he did want to check them out first.

He found a place where the undergrowth was thinner. After taking some rope from his pack, he tied both horses to trees, leaving enough slack so they could graze on a patch of grass. He slowly made his way around the valley, staying in the protective cover of the trees and underbrush. Occasionally, he stopped and studied the glade, trying to see where the voices were coming from. Soon he spotted a caravan wagon sitting under a spreading maple tree. All around it were other indications of human habitation—clothing hung on bushes to dry, a campfire that had burned down to a few coals, and a horse staked near the wagon. Lowell was glad he was good at tracking and keeping quiet or the horse would have already announced his presence.

If he remembered right, and he was sure he did, the waterfall was on the other side of the tree where the wagon sat, just through some underbrush. He glanced in that direction and saw two figures coming through the trees. They were talking and laughing, but he couldn't see them very well. He couldn't understand anything they were saying, either, but they had to be young, because their voices weren't deep yet. They were dressed in shirts and trousers, and their dark hair made their faces stand out. If only he were close enough to see their features, but they were a light blur in the shadows.

When the two emerged into the sunlight, Lowell could tell they were women. Evidently, they had been in the pool or under the waterfall, because their long black hair glistened with water as it hung down their backs. They walked over to the bushes where the clothes had been spread. One of the women removed what was there while the other woman began to spread more to dry.

Lowell felt like an invader. He wondered if any men were with the women, but he doubted it. They were dressed in shirts and trousers themselves. If they were traveling alone, they probably tried to pass themselves off as young men to protect themselves from unwanted attention. Lowell wondered what their story was. He tried to decide whether to approach them or find another place to camp. Just then, one of the women danced across the clearing with her hands raised to the sky. His attention was drawn to the other one, who stood quietly watching her.

When he looked back at the exuberant one, he was shocked. If he didn't know better, Lowell would have thought she was Rissa Le Blanc. Drying tendrils of curly hair danced in the air around her head. She was close enough for him to see her face clearly. He shrank back deeper into the shadows and slipped completely behind a large tree trunk. He took a deep breath and peeked again.

"Marissa, the sun feels so good after the cool water." She whirled to look back at the other woman. "Come join me. We can walk instead of dance if you want to."

Lowell felt as if he had been kicked in the chest by his horse. Marissa. Rissa could be short for that. But she had called the other woman Marissa. Was this her sister? How could they look so much alike? Unless they were twins.

He leaned against the tree with his hands on his knees. What was going on here? Should he approach these women? And where was Le Blanc?

Lowell slid down the trunk until he was sitting on the ground. He took a deep breath and bowed his head while dangling his arms across his raised knees. *Now would be a good time for You to talk to me,* Gud. *What am I supposed to do?*

☙

Marissa knew how tired Clari was of this isolation. She did everything she could to make their time together exciting, but Clari had gone too far this time. Dancing in the sunshine. Marissa supposed she had to join her. Their skin needed to be the same shade for the game to work. Maybe she should just stay in the shade. If Clari were too tan, perhaps Pierre would call off the plan. Marissa knew that wasn't a possibility, but it felt good to think so.

This time when they were together, the sisters had talked more than they had ever done before. It was the first time Marissa told Clari what was deep in her heart. She wished they could just drive the wagon into Litchfield and tell their friends who they were. Gerda and Anna would understand, wouldn't they? But what about Lowell and Ollie? Ollie was as important to Clari as Lowell was to her. Would telling them the truth destroy their fragile friendships? Marissa would never know. Pierre would see to that. As soon as the plan was executed, they would leave town, never to return again. If only there were a God who could take away her sins. Then maybe she would have a chance. But Pierre dashed that hope every time she tried to voice it.

Raising her hands above her head, she stepped into the sunlight and slowly turned around. Clari was right. It felt good to move around in the light and warmth, but Marissa could never move with the reckless abandon of her sister, even if they were alone in this obscure wilderness.

&

Lowell sat still for a few minutes until a thought dropped into his mind. If he were to show himself, he probably would scare the young women. They might not even wait to see who he was. He had noticed a rifle leaning against the tree beside the wagon. They might shoot him in their haste.

He made his way back to the horses, took a long swig from his canteen, and untied them. He led the pack animal over to his horse, mounted him, then headed toward the slight trail that led in the direction of the clearing. He rode along as if he didn't know anyone was there—as if he were a hunter who happened on the valley.

He didn't look up until he was completely out of the trees and in the sunlight. Then he glanced around as if he were hunting for a place to camp. The young women still cavorted around the clearing. His horse saw the one staked near the caravan and whinnied.

The other horse raised its head and perked its ears, and the two young women stood as still as statues. After a moment, they turned and looked in his direction; then they ran into the shelter of trees beside their wagon.

"Hallo!" he shouted.

The women continued their headlong plunge into the shadows. One grabbed the rifle as she ran past. They took a position behind the wagon, and with the barrel of the rifle protruding, one leaned her head out so she could watch his approach.

"I'm not going to bother you," he called out when he was closer. "I've been hunting and need to get some fresh water from the waterfall. I won't disturb you." He continued to ride past the campsite.

One of the young women stepped out from behind the wagon. She still carried the rifle, but it wasn't raised so high. "Lowell Jenson, is that you?" The other young woman stepped up beside her.

Lowell stopped near them. He took off his hat and looked down at one of the women. "Rissa Le Blanc?" He glanced at the other one. "Or are you Rissa Le Blanc?"

In the face of the second young woman, he recognized the one he had been dreaming about. That hint of hurt was still in her eyes. Sky blue eyes surrounded by a smudge of long black lashes. She quickly averted her face but not before he noticed her slight smile.

The first woman still pointed the rifle at him, but he dismounted and stood beside his horse, patting his neck, watching them from the corner of his eyes. He didn't want to spook the young woman into pulling the trigger.

"Where is Pierre?"

The women turned to each other, a look of fear in their eyes. The one with the rifle stiffened.

"Why do you want to know?" she asked, her voice trembling.

Lowell faced them. "I was just wondering. I don't want to

disturb you, though." He continued to hold his horse's reins and the lead line to the pack animal. "I just wanted to camp here, but if that isn't all right with you, I won't. I do need some fresh water for myself and my horses." He continued walking toward the stream that led from the pool at the base of the waterfall. He forced himself not to look back at the two young women.

❧

Marissa heard the horse's whinny, and her heart started to pound wildly. Then she saw a man riding toward them. Clari grabbed her hand and pulled her toward the wagon. When he spoke, Mari was surprised. The voice she had grown to love, the voice that echoed in her memory, was there in the campsite with them. Could it really be Lowell Jenson?

Even though she couldn't look at him after she and Clari stepped away from the wagon's protection, Marissa was happy to see him. She watched him longingly as he led his horses toward the pool; then she looked at her sister.

"What will we do, Clari?"

Clari turned toward her sister. "I don't know. If we aren't hospitable to him, he will wonder why, but Pierre would be angry if he found out."

Marissa looked at the place where the man and two horses had disappeared into the shadows. "Clari, it's Lowell."

"Yes, I know, but now he knows there are two of us. What if he tells someone?"

"He won't hurt us."

Clari looked worried. "We have to tell him something when he returns from the waterfall. But what?"

"I wish we could tell him the truth." Marissa couldn't keep from glancing in the direction he had gone. "Maybe we could."

"No!" Clari's whisper was almost a shout.

ten

Lowell had more on his mind as he headed home than he did when he left. The short time he'd spent with the twins filled his head—and heart—with a myriad of questions. At least he knew there were two girls. Come to think of it, he still didn't know their names, except that one of them was Marissa. They were evasive and ill at ease while he was there, so he didn't prolong his visit. The story they told him was nothing short of incredible. Incredible and unbelievable. Unbelievable and probably a lie.

The girl whose name was Marissa didn't look him in the eye as they were telling their wild tale. He wished she had. He could hardly wait to get to the farm and talk to Ollie. But first he was going by town to ask August for a favor.

Lowell made good time getting to Litchfield. He stopped outside the blacksmith shop and tied his horse close to the watering trough. Lowell was glad no other horses were tied there. Maybe his future brother-in-law was alone.

When Lowell stepped through the door into the shadowy interior of the shop, he took off his hat and used it to fan himself. The summer heat was bad enough without getting close to the blazing forge. He didn't know how August could stand it.

August looked up from the plow he was shaping. "What brings you here this time of day?"

"I need to ask a favor."

August set the plow on the dirt floor, laid his tools on the workbench, then rubbed his hands on his jeans. "What do you need?"

Lowell combed his fingers through his hair. He didn't want to tell August too much, but he also didn't want him to be suspicious. "I want Ollie to go somewhere with me, and we need someone who is familiar with the farm to look after the animals. I know it's asking a lot, but could you do that for us?"

"Sure." August crossed his arms over his massive chest. "How long are we talking about?"

"Maybe just today, maybe longer."

"I don't have a lot of work right now. Let me bank the fire in the forge, and I'll ride out with you." August started toward the blaze. "You can show me what I need to do."

Lowell turned his hat around and around in his hands. "We'll be really grateful."

❧

Ollie looked out at the sound of horses' hooves and saw Lowell and August riding up to the barn door. He laid aside the saddle he'd been cleaning and stepped out into the sunlight.

"Lowell, what are you doing back so—?"

"I need you to go somewhere with me," his brother said quickly, interrupting him. "August will take care of the animals while we're gone. I'll tell you about it on the ride. Just saddle your horse, and we'll head out. I have enough provisions for both of us."

Lowell showed August what needed to be done while Ollie prepared his horse for travel. Within minutes, the brothers were heading northwest away from the farm.

When they were out of sight, Ollie pulled up under the shade of a tree in a small grove. "Are you going to tell me what's happening? I'm not riding any farther without an explanation."

Both brothers dismounted and tied their horses to a tree. Lowell walked over and sat on a fallen log near the horses. Ollie followed him but remained standing.

"You're not going to believe what I have to tell you." Lowell got a faraway look in his eyes. "I went up that canyon where *Far* took us camping that time, just before we started raising horses. You remember, near the waterfall."

Ollie nodded.

"When I reached the clearing in the forest, someone was camping there. I was afraid it was outlaws, but it wasn't. It was two beautiful young women."

"What are you talking about? What young women?"

Lowell stood and paced near his brother. "Rissa Le Blanc has a twin sister. Both of them were there."

Ollie dropped to the log. "Okay, come sit down and tell me about it."

Lowell lowered himself to the log. "They have a caravan wagon, a horse, and a rifle. And they were dressed in shirts and trousers. Le Blanc was nowhere around."

Ollie's eyes widened. "What were they doing there?"

"Well, that's where the story gets weird. They told me a tale about their being twins. One doesn't live here. She's been in New Orleans. But she came to visit her sister. They wanted time together, and Le Blanc took them out there in the wilderness to get to know each other better. He's coming back in a week or so to get them. Supposedly, the one from New Orleans will return there when he gets back, and he and Rissa will come to Litchfield."

Ollie quickly stood to his feet. "That doesn't make any sense."

"I know." Lowell stood again and brushed off the back of his trousers. "The sister called Marissa is like the Rissa I know. The other one is more like the Rissa you know."

Ollie stared at his brother.

"Do you think one of them has been out there all the time—and they changed places sometimes?"

Lowell nodded. "It looks that way to me. I've never felt good about Le Blanc, and after I left the young women, I had more suspicions about him. The whole time I was in the clearing, I felt as if they were very disturbed about my being there. That they were hiding something. And Marissa wouldn't look at me."

Ollie let out a deep breath. "We have to find out what's going on."

Lowell started toward his horse. "That's what I thought. That's why I came to get you now. I want us to get there before they have time to run away. Somehow I have the feeling they're in trouble and need help."

"Well, what are we waiting for, Brother?"

❧

Marissa watched Lowell disappear into the trees. She wished she could have talked to him alone. Clari had done all the talking, and Marissa couldn't even look at his face. She hated lying to him. Now she had no hope he would ever be interested in her. She knew it was only a fairy-tale wish, but she had a hard time letting it go.

She turned to her sister. "What are we going to do?"

Clari usually had good ideas but not now. "I don't know." She dropped onto the top step of the caravan.

Marissa crossed her arms over her waist. "Do you think he believed us?"

"I don't know. I wish you had watched his face. You know

Lowell better than I do. Maybe you could have seen if he believed."

Marissa started wringing her hands. "Oh, Clari, I couldn't look at him and lie to his face."

"What do you mean? We've been lying to them all the time we've been here."

"But I didn't want to." Marissa rubbed her sweaty palms down the sides of her trousers.

Clari stood and looked at the place in the forest where they had last glimpsed Lowell and his horses. "Do you think I like to lie?"

"What if he comes back?"

"Pierre gave us a lot of money. Maybe we should leave. We could go to Wayzata and take a train somewhere."

For a moment, Marissa wished they could do what Clari suggested, but she knew it was no use. "And what would we do when we got there? Pierre said no one would give us a job. And I'm not going to. . .sell my. . .body as he said we would have to."

Clari rubbed her hand over her eyes. "Maybe we could teach school. Some small towns have a hard time getting a teacher. At least Mother made sure we could read, write, and work arithmetic. A lot of people don't know even that much."

Marissa clutched her sister's arm. "Pierre would find us. I know he would, and when he did, we would pay for running away."

"How long has he been gone? It's been over a week, hasn't it?"

Marissa nodded.

"Maybe everything is okay. Lowell probably went somewhere else to camp, and he won't bother us again."

"I hope you're right." Marissa shook her head. "I really hope you are."

❧

Ollie followed Lowell down the gully into the canyon that led to the valley around the waterfall. His mind was filled with memories. Even though it had been years since Father had brought them there, he remembered every detail with clarity. He and Lowell had laughed and pretended to be outlaws while they followed their father. Although Father was often a stern man, he seemed amused by the boys' antics. These vivid scenes playing through his mind brought tears to Ollie's eyes. He wished Father were with them today. He would help them know what to do when they reached the valley.

Soon they arrived where Lowell had left the packhorse. He pulled up the stake and put it back in the pack; then he took the horse's lead and set off through the thick forest, with Ollie following.

By the time they rode out of the trees, it was nearing dusk. Ollie saw the caravan sitting under a tree with a horse hobbled nearby but no sign of the young women. The two men rode slowly across the clearing, scanning the area.

Ollie wondered why he had never come back to this peaceful place. A gentle breeze sighed through the trees, and he could hear birds settling down for the night and small animals moving around. Even the horse near the wagon seemed calm and not alarmed at their arrival, perhaps because of Lowell's visit earlier that day.

Lowell stopped with Ollie beside him.

"What do we do now?"

Lowell dismounted, then looked at him. "We wait. They have to be here somewhere."

Within minutes, the two young women came from the

direction of the waterfall. Even though they wore shirts and trousers, they didn't resemble men. Ollie had never seen a woman in trousers. The girls didn't look as feminine as he thought they should, but they were still beautiful.

They were talking animatedly and didn't notice the two men. Then suddenly they stopped, their eyes wide. One sister stepped behind the other, and the one in front moved forward.

"Lowell—Ollie, how nice to see you."

Ollie tipped his hat. "Rissa—or whatever your name is."

The girl blushed. "My name is Clarissa." She gestured toward the other woman. "This is my sister, Marissa."

Marissa didn't look at him.

Clarissa turned toward Lowell. "Why did you come back?"

Lowell kept staring at Marissa, but she refused to look up.

"We'd like to camp in this meadow. Perhaps we could set up our campsite a little ways from yours. We could share one fire—maybe even our supper." He glanced at Clarissa.

Clarissa's cheeks flushed scarlet. She looked at Ollie, then back at Lowell.

"How long will you be staying?" Her voice trembled.

Couldn't Lowell see how uncomfortable she was? Ollie wanted to intervene, but he didn't.

"Probably just for one night," Lowell told Clarissa, then looked back at Marissa.

"Pierre may come back soon. He won't like it." She was beginning to sound like the Rissa Ollie remembered.

"Do you expect him tonight?" Lowell stood with his arms crossed over his chest.

Ollie was sure his brother intimidated the young women. Why couldn't he let up a little?

"No." The soft reply came from the woman named

Marissa. She was looking at Lowell. "He won't be back tonight. Maybe not for a few days."

Lowell unfolded his arms and stuck his hands in his back pockets. "Then we'll be gone before he returns."

❧

Lowell was glad when Marissa and Clarissa agreed to let them bed down close by. It didn't take long to set up their camp. Then he and Ollie gathered wood to make a fire.

The brothers cooked their canned beans while the sisters prepared their meal. Lowell opened a tin of peaches and offered another tin to the young women.

"Thank you," Clarissa said, taking the can. "We've made enough biscuits, if you'd like some."

They sat around the campfire and began to eat.

Lowell smiled and leaned forward. "I don't want to hurt you, but Ollie and I don't believe the story you told me this morning."

The sisters stopped eating and glanced at each other; then Marissa turned toward him. He saw again the pain in her eyes and wanted to take her in his arms and comfort her.

Marissa lowered her head. "You're right. It was a lie." She looked up into his eyes. "I never wanted to lie to you, Lowell."

The soft timbre of her voice went straight to his heart, melting it. Lowell moved closer to her.

"Marissa, I know something is wrong here." He took her hand. "And I think it has to do with your father."

She pulled her hand away and stood quickly. "He's not my father!" Then she clapped her hand over her mouth and looked at her sister with tears in her eyes.

Clarissa pulled her into her arms and patted her back. "It's all right, Mari." Clarissa looked over her sister's shoulder at

Lowell. "Now see what you've done!"

Marissa stepped away. "Don't blame Lowell. It's all Pierre's doing." The two women stared at each other. "We've wondered if our new friends in Litchfield would understand. Now would be a good time to find out."

Clarissa shook her head. "No. Pierre would be very angry."

Ollie stood up and turned toward Clarissa. "Who is Le Blanc, and what kind of hold does he have on you?"

Marissa covered her face with her hands and burst into tears.

"Hush, Sister," Clarissa said gently, holding her and patting her back again. "It will be all right. It must be."

Marissa finally stopped crying, and the two women walked over to the woods, then disappeared among the trees.

"I think it's time for us to pray for them," Lowell said, bowing his head.

* * *

Tonight Ollie was glad Lowell wasn't talkative. His own thoughts occupied him. He finished praying and watched the woods, hoping the girls were safe. It was dark now. They'd probably been here long enough to know how to get around at night. He looked up. The moon and stars shone brightly overhead, illuminating the dark sky, but even with the brilliance the shadows of the grove might obscure a tree root or something else they could trip on. He was about to search for them when they stepped into the circle of light.

Clarissa led the way to the side of the campfire opposite where the two men waited. "We've decided we can trust you. We'll tell you what you want to know." Marissa stood behind her and nodded. "We are Clarissa and Marissa Voss. Pierre is our stepfather."

Clarissa Voss. Ollie liked the sound of that name much

better than the one she used when he first met her. "So why did you call yourselves Rissa Le Blanc?"

Clarissa looked at him. "Pierre thought we should go by Rissa when we were in town, because it's part of both our names. We never told anyone our last name was Le Blanc. People assumed it was, and Pierre forbid us to say otherwise."

Lowell frowned. "What kind of hold does Le Blanc have on you?" His voice sounded harsh as he repeated Ollie's earlier question.

Marissa stepped up beside her sister. When she spoke, her voice was gentler. "Why don't we all sit down? Clari and I will tell you the whole story."

The brothers had pulled two logs near the fire before supper, and now they sat opposite the girls on the logs.

"We came from a Southern family," Marissa explained.

Lowell chuckled. "We could tell that."

Marissa smiled. "Our family owned a large plantation before the War between the States."

Ollie had learned about the war through studying history in school and from the stories his father told them.

"Somehow our family retained the plantation throughout the war," Clarissa added. "Our grandfather was able to run it, hiring workers to help him. When our mother and father married, Father took over the plantation."

"I remember wonderful times with our father before he died." Marissa was staring into the fire. "He was tall, and he loved us very much."

"But he died when we were young." Clarissa went on with her story, ignoring the interruption. "When we were about seven years old, Grandfather sold the plantation, and we moved to a large house in New Orleans with him and our mother."

"So New Orleans wasn't exactly a lie." Lowell stared at

Marissa until she looked at him and shook her head. Lowell smiled. "I'm glad."

Ollie saw something pass between them. He glanced at Clarissa, and she was staring at him. He smiled. Oh, yes, this was the woman he remembered.

Clarissa cleared her throat. "Grandfather died after we moved into town. It wasn't long before Mother met Pierre. He swept her off her feet, and they were married soon after that. I think she was just lonely. Then, about two years later, Mother contracted malaria. She never recovered."

"Actually, that was a blessing," Marissa said. "She didn't know Pierre was a confidence man. If she had lived longer, I don't think he would have been able to hide it from her." Marissa gave a deep sigh. "But he inherited what was left of the family fortune—and us."

Ollie stood and stuffed his hands in his front pockets. "Didn't you have any other family to take care of you?"

Clarissa shook her head, and her abundant black curls swirled around her shoulders. Ollie liked her hair hanging free, instead of up in an elaborate style. He could just imagine how soft it must feel.

"It didn't take Pierre long to go through the fortune. I think he gambled it away." Clarissa looked at Marissa, who had her head down. "He sold the house, and we started moving around the country. We were only twelve years old then. He said he'd worked out the 'greatest confidence game of all.' He forced us to do what he wanted. If we tried to rebel, he beat us."

Lowell slammed his fist against the log and jumped up. "Why didn't anyone stop him?" He looked from one sister to the other.

"Oh, he never left bruises where anyone could see them," Marissa said. "After we were older, he quit striking us."

"Because I stood up to him," Clarissa said.

Her sister nodded. "But he threatened to sell us into. . .a house of. . .ill repute if we didn't do what he wanted."

Lowell paced away from the fire and stood gazing up at the starry sky.

He turned back to the girls. "So what is this 'greatest confidence game of all'?"

Clarissa put her head in her hands, rubbed her face, then answered. "He takes one of us into a town and leaves the other in a remote campsite. Sometimes he switches us so we both have a chance to be in town."

"But I usually prefer being in the camp because I like to read," Marissa said.

Lowell turned to her, a look of compassion on his face.

"While Pierre is getting to know 'all the right people,' he is scouting possible places for us to rob. Then when a big event happens, which most of the people attend, he takes me with him to the event." Clarissa glanced at Marissa.

"And I rob the places he has told me to." Marissa dropped her head into her hands and sobbed again.

Lowell walked over to her and gently put his hands on her shoulders.

"If anyone happens to see Marissa and comes to the hotel to arrest me, Pierre has many witnesses to the fact that he and I were at the event. We leave town at once and never return."

Ollie looked at Lowell, his brother's face reflecting his own shocked feelings. The poor women. "How long has this been going on?"

Clarissa stood. "Almost eight years."

"Eight years!" Ollie exclaimed. "How many towns have you been to?"

Clarissa turned away from him and sighed. "I don't know.

At least two or three a year—maybe more some years."

Anger welled up inside Ollie. How could that man have done this? It was a wonder the women weren't ruined. "What about the friends you've made? Didn't anyone try to help you?"

Marissa finally looked up. Trails of tears still stained her cheeks. "We've never made friends before. Pierre kept us away from people. He'd always tell them he's very protective of his daughter, and they believed him." She stood beside her sister. "You two and Gerda and Anna are the only friends we've had since Mother died."

Ollie shuddered to think what could have happened to them. He thanked God for bringing them to Litchfield. Somehow he and Lowell had to rescue them from Le Blanc. The women had been held captive by his evil mind.

eleven

Lowell and Ollie camped far enough away from the young women so as not to bother them, but they kept the other camp in sight. They wanted to protect Clarissa and Marissa, if the need arose during the night. They spread their bedrolls close together on the ground, then lay down on them without taking off their boots.

Lying on his back, Lowell gazed up at the stars. He was tired, but he couldn't sleep. His mind went over and over the story he had heard that evening. It was more fantastic than the lie the young women had told him earlier, but he believed every word. Marissa looked at him while she talked, and he could read the sincerity in her gaze. His heart nearly broke when the twins relayed all that had transpired in their lives since their mother died. He knew it wasn't right to want to hurt anyone, but if Le Blanc had been there, Lowell probably would have done so. What kind of man used young women for his own ill-gotten gains? No kind of man. He had no conscience. He and his brother had to devise a scheme for helping the Voss sisters escape from him.

"Ollie." Lowell kept his voice low.

"Yes?"

"Ah. You can't sleep, either?"

"No. We have to help them." Ollie raised his head and leaned on one elbow. "I've been trying to figure out a way."

Lowell sat up and crossed his legs. "Whatever we do, we need to do it soon."

Ollie moved to a sitting position also. "I believe the sheriff would take into consideration the fact that they were forced to do what they did."

Lowell nodded. "I'm sure he would too."

A gentle breeze started blowing across the prairie grass that filled the large clearing, bringing welcome relief from the heat of the day. It had not cooled down much after sundown. Lowell turned his face into the wind. Just then, a rustling in the grass caught his attention. In the bright moonlight, he glanced at a place where the grass was moving more than anywhere else. He glimpsed the light glinting off shiny fur. Probably some nocturnal animal out foraging for food. Lowell watched it disappear into the underbrush.

"I'd like to talk to the sheriff. What do you think?" Ollie asked.

Lowell turned to his brother. "That's a good idea. But when?"

"Well, I can't sleep. I think I'll go now."

"Sheriff Bartlett will be asleep." Lowell chuckled. "He might not like you waking him in the middle of the night."

Ollie stood and straightened his clothes. "I think this is important enough to wake him. Besides"—he glanced toward the other camp—"I think we should do something before Le Blanc returns. Every minute we waste might be dangerous for them."

Lowell stood, then placed his hand on his brother's shoulder. "Just be careful. It's dangerous to ride across unfamiliar territory in the dark." He hesitated. "I'm glad the problem between us was just a misunderstanding. I'll be praying for you while you're gone. I don't expect to get any sleep, either."

❧

Ollie walked his horse the short distance to the tree line; then he mounted the horse and let him pick his way through the underbrush. Dark shadows made it harder, but while he rode, he prayed for protection. Once out of the forest, he stepped up the pace, though he still had to be careful on the uneven, rocky ground through the canyon and gully.

When he arrived at Litchfield, it looked like a sleeping town. The only lights were down the street at the saloon. He made his way up Main Street to the sheriff's office and jail. Bartlett, a widower, lived in a room behind the office. Ollie went around the building and tapped on the darkened glass of the window. He waited a few minutes, then tapped again. Immediately after the second tap, he saw a kerosene lamp flare, then Bartlett holding the lamp by the window. He motioned to Ollie to go around to the front.

"What brings you here at this time of night, Ollie?" The sheriff closed the door behind him. "Is there a problem at the farm?"

Ollie shook his head. "It's something else. I'm sorry to bother you at this hour, but I thought it was important."

The sheriff eased into the chair behind his desk. Ollie sat across from him; then he began to relate to him what the Voss sisters had told him and his brother. Bartlett leaned back in his chair and listened carefully.

At the end, the sheriff sat forward and looked him in the eyes. "Do you believe the story?"

Ollie nodded. "When Lowell first saw them this morning, they told him a lie; but later, when he took me back, we were able to convince them to trust us."

The sheriff chuckled. "I'm sure you were. So where is Le Blanc now?"

"I don't think the twins know for sure. He left them in the camp and said he had some business to attend to. He told them he'd be back in a couple of weeks."

"Twins." The sheriff scratched the stubble on his jaw. "That's really something, isn't it?"

Ollie stood and walked over to the desk. "The robbery will take place when the circus comes."

Sheriff Bartlett looked up at him. "That would be a good time. Most of the people in town will attend the performance. It's the first time the circus has ever been in Litchfield. It's not long off, is it?"

"I know. That's why I didn't wait until morning to see you."

The sheriff stood and opened the bottom desk drawer. He withdrew his gun belt and strapped it around his hips.

"Um, there's one other thing." Ollie stuck his hands in his front pockets. "Clarissa and Marissa don't know I've come to see you. Lowell and I wondered if you could somehow arrange to keep from prosecuting them if they help you capture Le Blanc."

The sheriff grabbed his hat off the hook by the door, shoved it on his head, then turned back to Ollie. "Let me think about that on the ride. How far did you say they were from town?"

⁂

Dawn was peeking over the treetops when Clarissa heard horses coming through the woods. She had dozed off and on all night. In one way, she felt as if a burden had been lifted from her shoulders. But she was also afraid of what would happen now. She thought she could trust Lowell and Ollie, especially Ollie. What if she was wrong? What if their decision to be truthful backfired and they ended up in prison? Would that be any worse than the life they were living? For the first time since she had become an adult, she knew what it meant to have friends. If that was taken away from her and Mari, it might as well be prison.

Two men burst through the trees across the clearing and headed straight toward their camp. In the dim light of early morning, she recognized Ollie. Where had he gone this early? And who was the other rider? She could see Lowell moving around the campsite across the way. For a moment, she was afraid it was Pierre. But why would he be riding with Ollie, and where was the wagon? She shaded her eyes from the rays of the rising sun to get a better view.

"Who's that?" Mari spoke from just behind her.

Clarissa whirled around. "I don't know who the other one is, but Ollie is one of them."

"Then everything is all right, isn't it?"

As they drew closer, Clarissa noticed the other man was wearing a star on his shirt. Her heart dropped like a rock in the pool at the base of the waterfall, and she felt as if she were drowning. What had Ollie done? Had he turned them in to the sheriff? She hoped Marissa didn't notice, but when her sister grabbed her shoulders, she could feel her trembling.

"Oh, Clari, it's the sheriff." Mari's voice caught on a sob. "What are we going to do?"

Ollie dismounted and started toward her. She glared at him, and he quickened his pace.

"Don't worry, Clarissa. Everything's going to be all right."

His whispered words did nothing to calm the storm raging inside her.

The sheriff was an older man with kind, clear blue eyes, but Clarissa knew he wouldn't go easy on criminals. She had heard about him while she was in town.

Lowell walked over to him. "Sheriff Bartlett. Good to see you." The older man extended his hand, and Lowell shook it.

Clarissa wanted to scream at them. Everyone was being

polite, and she was worried about her future—hers and Mari's. She wished they would dispense with the pleasantries and get to the point. Were they going to jail—or not?

"Sheriff, I want you to meet Clarissa and Marissa Voss." Ollie gestured to each woman.

The sheriff reached up and tipped his hat. "Ladies."

Clarissa looked at him. "So, Sheriff, why are you here?"

"I want you to tell me your story. Then we'll see where we go from there."

Clarissa let out a little breath; then, with her sister's help, they both related the story. Mari's voice trembled at first, as did Clarissa's, but soon they relaxed. Clarissa watched the sheriff. He kept his gaze focused on the one who was talking—never showing any emotion, positive or negative.

When they were finished, he cleared his throat. "Well, now we have a situation here, don't we?"

Clarissa wondered what he meant by that.

"I think I can be of help to you, if you will help me."

"What do you mean?" Clarissa asked, almost feeling hopeful.

"If you will help us catch Le Blanc in the act, we won't prosecute you. Even though you've committed many crimes, I believe you when you say he forced you. I'd like to put him behind bars."

And I'd like to help you. Clarissa let out a deep sigh. The sheriff believed them and was offering a way out of their bondage to Pierre. She smiled and looked at her sister. Mari nodded. Clarissa turned back to the sheriff. "Just tell us what we have to do."

The women sat down with the sheriff and the two brothers and planned how they would catch Pierre. They decided it would need to be during the robbery or when he had the stolen goods. After awhile, the three men mounted their horses and rode toward the forest. Near the trees, Lowell turned and made his way to his camp. He loaded the supplies onto the packhorse, then rode off with the sheriff and Ollie. Clarissa wondered what Ollie and the sheriff had talked about while they waited for Lowell.

Just before he disappeared into the trees, Ollie looked back at the camp where she and her sister waited. She returned his wave and felt a sense of loss when he was gone. It had only been two days, but she had relaxed around him more than she had in town. She hoped that when this was over they could get to know each other better.

෨

It was nearing dusk later that day when Pierre rode up in the wagon. Marissa was glad he hadn't come any sooner.

"Pierre, you're back. It hasn't been two weeks yet."

"Aren't you glad to see me, Marissa? I just couldn't stay away from my two lovely daughters any longer." His laugh echoed in the open stillness around them.

All evening, Pierre would start sentences, then stop midway and laugh, a gleam in his eyes, as if he had a secret. Marissa didn't care. She didn't want to know anything about him or where he'd been. She was sure he'd spent part of the time with unsavory companions, some of them women. How she hated him and what he had done to her. She imagined her life would have been much like that of Gerda or Anna if she'd never known him. Maybe it wasn't too late. She certainly hoped not. But Pierre wasn't the only one with a secret, and the one she and Clari shared would put him in prison. It was hard for her to act natural around him. She was glad when he said Clarissa would be going into town with him this time. It would be easier to wait at the camp for the fateful day. The only thing

Marissa regretted was that she would have to commit one more crime, but it would be the last. And Pierre would be out of their lives forever, she hoped.

twelve

It was the last day of August, and the circus train was coming that morning. The railroad agent had posted a sign to let everyone know when it was due. By the time they could hear the huge mechanical monster in the distance, chugging toward the station, gawkers crowded the platform. Others were scattered along both sides of the tracks. Young mothers sat on the benches beside the depot, holding toddlers and babies. Children darted in and out among the crowd as though they were playing hide-and-seek with each other, and the more daring boys stood at the edge of the platform and hung out over the tracks to wait for the engine's approach.

Ollie leaned against the depot wall, watching the activity. Lowell was taking his turn at keeping watch on Marissa in the camp. Of course, she didn't know he was there, but the brothers had decided they wouldn't leave her alone in the wilderness.

Ollie scanned the crowd, looking for Clarissa. He didn't see her, but Le Blanc was there, watching everything with a huge smile on his face. The excitement would help his scheme succeed. Ollie glanced down Main Street. Since most of the people who were in town were at the station, the thoroughfare looked deserted, except for the shop owners who stood near their doors in case a stray customer needed an item. Even the saloon keeper and a few of the women sauntered toward the tracks and clustered in small groups a short distance from the crowd. At least the women were dressed modestly. It was a wonder they were awake this early since they'd worked so late at night.

"The train's here!" someone shouted. "I can see it coming!"

Smoke belched from the smokestack on the powerful engine, and cars spread down the track as far as the eye could see. More than fifty long railroad cars, Ollie guessed.

When the whistle blew, the stationmaster made his way out onto the platform and tried to get the crowd to move back. Finally, the sheriff and his deputy came to help him. Within moments, the people had moved to a safer distance, and the stationmaster stepped up beside the huffing engine as its shrieking brakes brought it to a halt. He spoke to the engineer, then directed him to move to a side track that ran beside the main line. After all the cars were on the other track, he turned the wheel that threw the switch, leaving the tracks ready for the next train to pass through town.

People emerged from the railroad cars and moved quickly to perform their duties.

The ringmaster, in a uniform covered with gold braid and fringe, lifted a megaphone to his mouth. "Come one, come all—to the greatest spectacle you've ever seen! At precisely two o'clock, the circus parade will begin!" He turned toward another part of the crowd. "Come see the performers and fee-ro-cious wild animals from the jungles of Africa! The parade will start at that end of Main Street." He swept his white-gloved hand down the street. "And it'll come this way and go out to the field beside Lake Ripley. See the greatest little show under the big top right after the parade!"

The clock on the depot chimed ten o'clock. Ollie guessed

it would take about four hours for the workers to set up the mammoth tent pictured on the flyers around town. He noticed Le Blanc leaning against the depot wall, writing in a notebook. Ollie wished he could see what he was writing, but he didn't want to alert the man to his interest.

After most of the people had dispersed from the area, Ollie decided to go home and get his mother. She might enjoy the excitement. He'd take her to eat at the hotel. Since he and his brother wouldn't be home at lunchtime, she probably wouldn't fix herself anything, either. Ollie was worried about her not eating right since Father died. Her clothes were beginning to hang on her thin frame. Perhaps someone else's cooking would perk up her appetite.

He figured she could spend a little time with Anna, then watch the parade with her from the front of the Dress Emporium. After that he'd try to get the two women to go with him to the performance. He wanted everything to seem normal to Le Blanc.

The hotel restaurant was crowded when Ollie arrived with his mother; but one group left, and they were given that table. His mother ate more than she had in some time. After dropping her off at his sister's store, Ollie sauntered up the street, stopping and talking to people as he went. Finally, he stepped into the sheriff's office, as if paying a friendly visit.

"Is everything all set?" Ollie asked Sheriff Bartlett.

Bartlett glanced out the window. "Yes, a friend sent several of his deputies to help us. They're already hidden in the forest around the campsite where the girls are. Mr. Finley told me he was closing the bank during the circus performance, so I asked if he and his family would sit with Le Blanc and his daughter."

"Did you tell him why?" Ollie hesitated. "I mean, do you think it's good for many people to know what's going on?"

"No, I didn't tell him, and I agree with you. But he has a daughter who might enjoy Clarissa."

After reviewing the plans, Ollie left the office and headed toward the bank. Le Blanc was just coming out of the door.

"Are you and Rissa going to the performance this afternoon?"

"We wouldn't miss it," Le Blanc said with a smile and continued down the street.

Ollie smiled to himself. *I'm sure you wouldn't.*

&

Clarissa couldn't believe her good fortune. Pierre had suggested she might like to watch the parade with her friends at the Dress Emporium, so he took her there right after an early lunch. He would get Mari and bring her to town, keeping her hidden in the wagon until after the circus performance started. Then she would rob the homes he had listed and return to the wagon to hide again.

I hope Ollie will come by the store while I'm there. She sighed as she remembered his green eyes and wavy brown hair. Soon after she arrived at the Dress Emporium, Ollie came, as well as his mother. She was a lovely older woman. Now Clarissa knew where Ollie got his good looks. He shared many of his features with his mother, even though her brown hair was laced with silver strands that only added to her beauty.

Clarissa watched Mrs. Jenson talking with her daughter and Gerda. How she wished she'd known her mother after she had reached adulthood. The special bond between these two women was evident. A mother would have made a big difference in the way her life and Mari's had turned out. Clarissa had to swallow the tears that clogged her throat. She didn't want anyone to guess anything was wrong. She tried to join in the pleasant conversation but had little to say. She was glad the other women were too busy talking to notice.

Soon it was time to move outside for the parade. The boardwalks were already filling with people. She was thankful no one was in front of the Dress Emporium yet. Gerda and Anna moved chairs from the store and set them under the awnings the Braxtons had recently added to the front of the building. The women would have a comfortable, shaded spot to watch the festivities.

A horse-drawn calliope led the parade. The music it played was lively and different from anything Clarissa had ever heard—tinny and breathy at the same time. Clowns and jugglers followed, then two men leading three huge gray animals. The handlers carried long sticks and walked on either side of the animals, keeping them in line down the middle of the street. A woman in a fancy costume perched on the neck of the first animal. The beasts' long trunks and huge ears swished through the air, stirring up a small breeze, and their feet raised giant puffs of dust that filled the air around them.

"What are those?" Clarissa whispered, staring at them. For the first time, she wished she'd been as interested in books as her sister. Mari would know what they were.

"They're elephants." Anna watched as the animals drew closer. "I saw a picture of one in a book once, but these are the first real ones I've seen."

Clarissa leaned as far back in her chair as she could. What

if an elephant stepped on her? It could kill her. But some boys dashed out into the street and tried to get as close as possible to them. One boy even reached out to touch one of the elephant's legs.

"You there, Boy!" one of the handlers barked. "Get back before he tramples on you!"

The boy jumped back on the boardwalk, his friends right after him.

Behind the elephants came horse-drawn wagons with colorful cages containing other strange animals. Some of them prowled around the cages and roared at the crowd. This seemed to excite some of the boys, but Clarissa didn't like it. The sound was terrifying, coming from such close proximity. In the heat of waning summer, the strong wild animal smells were almost overwhelming. She held a white handkerchief to her nose and didn't breathe very deeply.

After the caged animals passed, other performers wearing fancy costumes and heavy makeup rode horses or walked down the street, waving to the people who lined the thoroughfare. Clarissa wondered what they looked like under the garish greasepaint. Then she saw a man carrying a stick that was on fire. He had just reached the street in front of the Dress Emporium when he stuck the burning end into his mouth, then pulled it back out.

Clarissa gasped and shuddered. "Why did he do that?"

"He's a fire-eater," Anna said, her eyes wide. "I've read about them too, but I've never seen one." She looked from one end of the street to the other. "In fact, most of these things are new to me. I can hardly wait for the performance to start."

When the last of the parade had passed, Ollie returned for his sister and his mother, with Pierre close behind. He offered Clarissa his arm, then escorted her down the street toward the tent. She wished he'd waited until the dust from the parade had settled. She covered her nose again with the now-dingy handkerchief. A brown film blanketed everything.

Smaller tents and booths dotted the landscape around the big tent, and hawkers called out to the people to come inside and behold the "wonders" they boasted about. One was supposed to be a bearded lady, while another purported to house an Egyptian mummy.

The hawker outside one small tent shouted, "Step right up! Buy a ticket now! Inside this tent is General Tom Thumb and a gen-u-wine Feejee mermaid." He looked right at Pierre. "Come on, Sir—buy a ticket so you and your lady friend can see these amazing wonders!"

Pierre leaned close to her. "Would you like to see something before the show starts?"

Clarissa shook her head. With the closed tents and the heat, she didn't want to venture inside one, even to see a mummy or a mermaid. And she was appalled the man thought she was Pierre's lady friend.

"Perhaps you'd like a glass of lemonade?" Pierre stopped in front of a small wooden hut.

"Yes, anything to help my dry throat. Thank you."

Clarissa looked around her while Pierre paid for the drinks. She wondered how they'd set up everything in the time since the train had arrived that morning. Many people must have worked together. She sipped the cool liquid as they headed toward the main tent.

Inside she saw seats on raised platforms that looked like stairs around the perimeter of the tent. Sawdust covered the floor, and short barriers defined the different sections. Strange-looking equipment was attached to the tall poles that held up the great canvas, and most of the sides were rolled up to let in what little wind was blowing.

After buying two tickets, Pierre led her to a spot about halfway down one side of the long tent. "Would you like to sit on the front row?"

Clarissa shook her head. "No, not that close. Maybe farther back—up there in the second group of seats. We can still see over the heads of the people in front of us." They climbed up to the second tier, then sat down. Other seats along the rows were filling up, and a short time later, the banker, Mr. Finley, and his family joined them. Clarissa had never met Becky Finley, but soon they were chattering away as if they'd known each other for years.

Both old men and young strode up and down the aisles, calling out, "Roasted peanuts! Popcorn! Get 'em right here!" The atmosphere was festive—and different from anything Clarissa had ever experienced.

Circuses had traveled mainly in the East until recent years, so she and her sister had never been in the same town where one was performing. They would usually pull a con during a community barn dance, an Independence Day celebration, or a similar big event.

❧

Ollie escorted his mother into the tent and found seats where he could look straight across the center ring at Clarissa. Soon August brought Gerda and Anna to sit with them. Ollie knew they were talking, but his attention was trained on the woman sitting across the tent. Today her hairstyle was not as elaborate as usual. It reminded him of the way she looked out at the campsite. A ribbon the color of her dress tied back her hair, and her curls bounced against her shoulders as she moved her head. He gazed at her. *If only someday I could touch those curls. . .*

"Did you hear what I said, Ollie?"

His mother's voice brought him back to the present. "I'm sorry, Mother. I didn't."

"Do you think something will be happening in all three rings at once?"

"I don't know." He smiled at her. "But why else do you think they'd have three rings?"

Just then the ringmaster announced the equestrian events in ring number one. Riders circled the ring while executing tricks on the backs of the horses, sometimes standing, sometimes sitting. One even stood on his hands on the horse's back. Then suddenly, the ringmaster turned their attention to ring number three at the other end of the tent. A man stepped inside a large cage that held two lions and three tigers. He cracked a whip about their heads until they stood on small round pedestals.

"I want to watch both of them, but I can't." Mother looked first at one ring, then at the other.

Ollie smiled at her. He hadn't seen her this animated since Father had died. Maybe it would take her mind off losing him—for a short while anyway. Then Ollie glanced across the ring at Clarissa. She was watching the big cats. One of them roared, and she shuddered. Quickly, she turned to watch the performers on horses. He had never been to a circus, but he didn't want to waste any of the time he could spend appreciating her beauty.

"And now, ladies and gentlemen, turn your attention to the

center ring! Those masters of laughter are coming your way!" The ringmaster pointed to the clowns, tumbling and chasing each other into the ring.

Ollie glanced at Clarissa again. She was laughing and clapping her hands. He could feel his own heart tumbling too. Clarissa—so happy, so beautiful—took his breath away. He wanted to help her be happy for the rest of her life.

Ollie shook his head. He didn't know if she was a Christian, and he knew the Bible spoke plainly against a believer marrying an unbeliever. But he couldn't get rid of the thoughts that filled his head and heart. He hoped he would find out soon if she knew the Lord. For now he would pray.

After the clowns had cavorted around the center ring, the ringmaster announced the high-wire acts. "Oohs" and "aahs" and gasps of breath rippled through the audience as various performers crossed the high wire—walking, riding a bicycle, juggling, and carrying a variety of bulky items. Ollie watched a myriad of emotions cross Clarissa's face at the same time.

The final act took place on the flying trapezes. It was the most spectacular of all. Ollie couldn't keep from watching it, even though he stole glances at the beautiful face across the tent.

❧

Clarissa was glad when the performance was over. Just before the end of the display on the trapezes, she noticed Ollie across the tent from where she sat. How long had he been there? After that, she had a hard time staying focused on the performers. One time, when she glanced at him, he was looking straight at her. She felt as if they were the only two people in the tent. Everything around her faded, and she could hardly breathe. The death-defying heroics of the troop held no more attraction for her. Ollie Jenson filled her mind and heart. If only her life had been different. More like Anna's or Gerda's. Perhaps then they would have had a future together.

As soon as most of the people were out of the tent, Clarissa noticed the circus workers dismantling the equipment. "Do you know where they're going next?" she asked Pierre.

"According to the front man, they'll have to head south for the winter." He helped her climb down from the tier where they'd been sitting. "Most of the wild animals came from Africa, and it's hot there. They can't tolerate the winters this far north."

They followed the rest of the crowd that was headed toward the middle of town. Pierre made a point of greeting many people. Clarissa knew he wanted them to remember talking to him and seeing her. Then, if anyone saw Mari before she slipped away, he could assure them Rissa Le Blanc was indeed at the circus. There would be plenty of witnesses to that fact. She only hoped this would be the last time she and her sister had to go through this.

By the time Clarissa and Pierre reached the place where most of the businesses were, they saw the banker coming out of the sheriff's office. Mr. Finley was talking and gesturing while Sheriff Bartlett listened to him. Pierre hurried toward the boardinghouse and let Clarissa into her room then went back downstairs.

A few minutes later, Pierre knocked on the door to Clarissa's room, then stepped inside. "The sheriff wants to talk to you."

"Did he say why?"

"No, and I didn't ask." Pierre was pacing about the room,

clenching and unclenching his fists. "Hurry. I don't want to keep him waiting."

Clarissa crossed the room to peer into her looking glass. She had already rinsed off the thin layer of dust that had covered her face and hands. She tucked a stray curl behind her ear, then left with Pierre.

Sheriff Bartlett stood in the parlor downstairs and waited for them to sit down. "Mr. Le Blanc, I'm afraid someone saw your daughter leaving Mr. Finley's home while he was at the circus. When he arrived home, many of their valuables were missing—including his wife's jewelry. He's very upset."

Clarissa glanced at Pierre out of the corner of her eye. He was looking directly at the sheriff, a calm expression on his face.

"Did Mr. Finley say it was Rissa who robbed him?"

"No. Someone else saw her. He had already come by the office and told me. You see, she was wearing a black shirt and dark trousers. The person who saw her thought it was unusual for her to be dressed that way and for her to be at that house when most people in town were at the circus."

Pierre rose quickly. "Who told you these things?"

"I'm afraid I can't give you that information, but he was someone I trust." The sheriff also stood. He turned his hat round and round. "I'm afraid I'll have to take Miss Le Blanc down to the jail."

Clarissa rose to her feet then. "What?"

"I'm sorry, Miss. It has to be done."

If Clarissa hadn't known he was playing a part, she would have been frightened. "But I was at the circus too."

"Can anyone substantiate that?"

Pierre interrupted. "Yes, we sat beside the Finleys. Let's go to their house. You'll see that you're wrong."

When they arrived at the residence, everything went the way Pierre had planned it. The Finleys assured the sheriff that Clarissa had indeed sat beside them.

Pierre flew into the rage he had planned for the occasion. "I can't believe you would treat anyone this way! My daughter and I have been fine upstanding citizens while we've lived in your town. And this is the way you treat us? We won't stay in such a place!" He glared at the sheriff, then took Clarissa's arm. "Come, Rissa—we won't spend another night here."

thirteen

At the boardinghouse, Pierre sought out Mrs. Olson and told her what had happened.

"Oh, you poor dear." The older woman patted Clarissa's cheek. "How could they think such a thing about you?"

How, indeed? Clarissa knew how, and all this subterfuge made her sick. Of course, they thought she was the one. Mari looked just like her. Clarissa wished she could shout the truth so everyone would hear, but that wasn't part of the plan.

"You have been a gracious hostess, Mrs. Olson," Pierre said in a smooth voice. "If this hadn't happened, we would have been glad to stay here a long time. Wouldn't we, Rissa?"

Clarissa nodded. When this was over, she would never have to hear that hated name again. Rissa. Her name wasn't Rissa. Neither was Mari's. Soon they could tell people their real names.

After Pierre paid Mrs. Olson, they went to their rooms to pack their bags. Clarissa looked around the room. She had loved being here. So had Mari. This was the first time they'd lived in a real house since they left their family home in New Orleans. Even though it had only been a few weeks, it felt like home. Clarissa wondered what would happen after the sheriff arrested Pierre. Had he meant it when he said he wouldn't have to arrest her or her sister? What would they do until Pierre came to trial? What would they do after he was convicted and sent to prison? So many questions raced through her mind. She walked to the window and looked out at the peaceful, tree-lined street. She wished she could come back here and share this room with her sister.

They loaded their bags into the surrey and headed south out of town. When they could no longer see the outskirts of Litchfield, Pierre turned toward the northeast, pulled into a tight grove of trees, and stopped beside a wagon hidden in the underbrush.

"Marissa," he called out softly. "You may come out now."

Clarissa expected to see her sister climb out from under the tarp on the wagon. Instead, Mari stepped from behind the underbrush. While Pierre was unhitching one of the horses from the surrey and hooking it to the wagon, Mari led Clarissa to a small pool of water in the middle of the copse.

"It was too hot under the tarp in the wagon." Mari trailed her fingers in the cool water. "I stayed here while I was waiting for you. I could hear anyone who might be coming and hide in any number of places."

The sisters rested there a few minutes, then returned to find Pierre in a good mood.

"Marissa, I'll let you ride in the surrey with your sister." His eyes gleamed as he climbed onto the wagon seat.

Clarissa was sure he was proud of what he had pulled off today. They'd had to leave a town like this only a few times. Usually, no one saw Mari, and Clarissa and Pierre left at leisure. Pierre liked the excitement of playing out the whole confidence game. More than once, he had boasted of his superiority when they were this successful.

He scoured the area to make sure no one was around; then he drove the wagon out of the copse. Clarissa drove the surrey out behind him with her sister seated beside her.

"How did it go?" Mari whispered.

"We'll talk about it later," Clarissa whispered back.

"Oh, Clari, tell me about the circus," she said then eagerly.

During the journey to the forest and the bit of prairie concealed in its depths, Clarissa told her about the parade, the sideshows and refreshments, and the performances. Mari listened closely. Clarissa wished her sister could have been there. Mari had no doubt seen pictures of some of those things in the books she read and would have loved being there.

☙

Ollie watched Pierre leave town with Clarissa. From a safe distance, he followed the wagon and the surrey when they drove out of the grove of trees. He knew where they were going and could stay far enough away so Pierre wasn't aware of his presence. Soon after they entered the forest, Ollie made his way through the trees to the place where Lowell had camped while he watched over Marissa.

Although Ollie was stealthy, Lowell met him as soon as he drew near. "How did it go in town?"

"Just the way we planned." Ollie dismounted and tied his horse to a tree. "I talked to Sheriff Bartlett. He asked another sheriff to send some of his deputies to help him. They're hiding in the woods somewhere around here."

Lowell smiled. "I know where they are."

The two brothers made their way closer to the tree line so they could observe what was happening.

Pierre stopped the wagon near the caravan and started unloading the stolen goods. The two sisters pulled up beside the wagon. He was smiling and talking excitedly to the girls, holding up various items, turning them around, watching the sun glint off their surfaces.

Soon Pierre disappeared into the caravan and dragged out a couple of wooden trunks. He started packing some of the items into them. He had the two girls help him. It looked as if they were separating the goods according to kind. Ollie watched Pierre place sparkling pieces of jewelry in one trunk and silver items in the other.

Then Pierre climbed back into the caravan to replace one of the trunks, and Ollie scanned the edges of the forest. Deputies were coming through the underbrush. He glanced back toward the campsite, and Pierre was climbing down from the caravan. He picked up another trunk and turned to reenter the vehicle. Sheriff Bartlett stepped forward from the tree line, gun in hand.

"Pierre Le Blanc! Stop where you are!"

Pierre turned slowly around to see men with guns emerge from the forest and move toward the camp. His eyes widened, and his face drained of its color. His moustache even seemed to bristle. Ollie almost chuckled at the expression. He and Lowell were following the deputies.

"Put down the trunk and raise your hands." The sheriff advanced across the wide clearing with rapid strides.

Pierre set the wooden container on the ground and straightened. He glanced toward each of the girls. His eyes narrowed, and he scowled. He lifted his hand toward Clarissa. Ollie's stomach tightened. He wanted to drive his fist into the man's face. He had never felt that way about anyone before.

The sheriff shouted, "Hold it right there, Le Blanc!" Pierre stopped. "Clarissa and Marissa, move over near the trees."

Le Blanc's face darkened. The veins in his neck bulged, and his face turned red with rage.

Ollie and Lowell stopped near the twins, out of the way of the deputies but close enough to see what was happening.

Two deputies stepped to the other side of Le Blanc. One

pulled his hands down, and the other handcuffed them behind him. When the cuffs clicked shut, something seemed to snap inside Pierre. He turned to look at the young women.

"How could you do this to me, you ungrateful wretches?" he yelled. Then he spewed out words so vile no one should have to hear them. They ricocheted and echoed through the trees, disgusting Ollie and no doubt devastating Clarissa and Marissa.

"Let's get them out of here." Lowell put words to Ollie's thoughts.

Ollie glanced at the sheriff, who nodded. The brothers quickly moved the young women toward Lowell's campsite. Pierre's screeches followed them, and the twins covered their ears with their hands.

At the campsite, Ollie and Lowell didn't take time to pack. One of them could return in a day or two to retrieve their belongings. They needed to get the women elsewhere as fast as possible. Ollie mounted his horse and pulled Clarissa up onto his lap, and Lowell did the same with Marissa. They hurried through the forest away from the evil man, who was still filling the air with his poison.

fourteen

Lowell was relieved when he no longer could hear the foul words spilling forth from Le Blanc. As long as he heard even a faint sound of the man's voice, though, he felt heat rising within him. They emerged from the forest, with Marissa still cradled against his chest. He urged his mount forward; the sooner they arrived at home, the better. He glanced at Ollie. The grim look on his brother's face probably mirrored his own. They needed to get the young women to a safe place. They could talk to the sheriff later.

By the time they reached the farm, their horses had slowed, but Lowell could still feel Marissa shaking in his arms. During the wild ride, she hadn't raised her face from where it pressed against his shirt. But he didn't mind. Having her so close was wonderful. He wanted to protect her from harm and hoped he'd be allowed to do that very thing. Gud, *help me know what to do. Show me what Your will is in this matter.*

Mother stepped out onto the front porch, wiping her hands with the bottom of her large apron. Lowell had seen her do this many times but not since Father died. She didn't look as pale and wan as she had when Lowell left to guard Marissa in the forest. He wondered why.

She came down the steps and waited by the hitching post until both her sons halted their horses. "Who is this with you, Lowell? I recognize the girl with Ollie. This one looks just like her, but why is she dressed like a man?" She placed her hands on her hips. "What's going on, boys?"

Lowell patted Marissa's back. "It's okay. You're safe now," he murmured against her fragrant hair.

Marissa gazed up at him and slowly loosened her hold on his shirt. Then she glanced around her. "Where are we?"

"You're at my home. This is my mother." Lowell gestured toward the older woman, who smiled up at them.

His mother lifted her arms toward Marissa. The young woman slipped down into them, and Mother gathered her into a close hug. They walked over to Ollie's horse where Clarissa already stood on the ground.

Mother hugged her too. "I'm glad to see you again, Rissa." She turned and put an arm around each girl. "Come—let's go into the house, and you can tell me what this is all about."

Lowell smiled grimly at Ollie, then called to the women, "We'll take care of the horses and join you in a few minutes."

On the way to the stable, Lowell asked his brother, "So what's happened to *Mor?* She seems different."

Ollie chuckled. "I took her to the circus."

❧

Mrs. Jenson escorted the young women into the parlor. Clarissa wondered how much she knew about what had transpired.

The older woman looked from one sister to the other and smiled. "You're twins. If you were dressed alike, I couldn't tell you apart. Now which one is Rissa Le Blanc?"

Her friendly manner helped Clarissa relax. "Actually, I'm Clarissa Voss, and this is my sister, Marissa."

The change of the last name didn't seem to bother Mrs. Jenson. "Well, Clarissa and Marissa Voss, you are welcome in our home. How about some lemonade and pound cake?"

Marissa nodded to Clarissa.

"Yes, that would be nice." Clarissa rearranged her skirt. It was quite wrinkled from the day's activities.

Just as Mrs. Jenson returned with a tray containing a pitcher of lemonade, glasses, and cake, Ollie and Lowell walked through the door. Clarissa smiled at Ollie, and his eyes lit up, making him even more handsome. Riding away from that awful scene, she had felt so protected in his arms. She didn't want to leave them when they arrived at the farm. Clarissa knew he was just being nice, but she could pretend it meant more to him too.

"Sit down, boys, and join us." Mrs. Jenson smiled at her sons. "I'm sure it won't spoil your supper." She chuckled.

Lowell and Ollie told their mother what had happened since Lowell found Mari and Clarissa at the campsite. Was it only a few days ago? It seemed like an eternity. An eternity that had changed her life—for the better, she hoped.

Mrs. Jenson was shocked at the news her sons related and clucked over the girls like a mother hen protecting her chicks. Clarissa had feared people would believe she and Mari were as guilty as Pierre, but when Mrs. Jenson smiled, Clarissa remembered how much her own mother had loved her.

"I am so sorry about all this, Mrs. Jenson," Clarissa said softly. "We would understand if you didn't want us in your home, considering what Pierre forced us to do."

The older woman's eyes were moist as she turned to Clarissa. "Did you want to do the things that man made you do?"

"No! Of course not!" both sisters exclaimed at once.

"Oh, you poor dears." The compassion in Mrs. Jenson's voice went straight to Clarissa's heart, softening it. "I can't believe that awful man did such terrible things to you girls."

Marissa was usually the quiet sister. "He was good at

putting on an act. He was so believable he could have gone on stage. That's why he could get away with almost any confidence game he planned." She shuddered.

Mrs. Jenson turned toward her older son. "What's Sheriff Bartlett going to do about these precious girls?"

"We're not sure. We'll talk to him later."

"They'll stay right here until he tells us anything different." She nodded firmly.

Ollie crossed the room to his mother and hugged her. "I knew you would say that. Thank you, *Mor*."

❧

The next morning, the sheriff drove up in a wagon with a trunk in the back. Ollie walked out from the barn to meet him.

"I thought the girls might need this." Sheriff Bartlett lifted the trunk down from the wagon. "Should I take it into the house?"

Ollie relieved the older man of his burden and hefted the trunk onto his shoulders. "Come on—let's go in for a cup of coffee. *Mor* made cinnamon rolls for breakfast. She might have one or two left."

"Well, now, I won't turn down your mother's good cooking." He patted his stomach. "I don't get home cooking very often."

Lowell joined them on the porch and opened the door for his brother. Ollie set the trunk in the hallway, and the three men went to the kitchen, where his mother was teaching Clarissa and Marissa how to bake bread.

His mother turned around and smiled. "Welcome, Sheriff Bartlett—how nice to see you."

"Ollie said you might have some coffee and cinnamon rolls left from breakfast." He grabbed his hat from his head and held it in his hands. "I know what a good cook you are, Mrs. Jenson."

Ollie pulled up a chair for the sheriff, and they all sat around the large kitchen table.

"I thought you might need some more clothes," Sheriff Bartlett told the sisters, "so I brought out one of your trunks."

Both girls clapped their hands. "That is so thoughtful!" Clarissa said. "Mrs. Jenson loaned us some of her clothes, but she's a little taller than we are. It'll be nice to have our own things."

Ollie looked at the sheriff. "What's happened to Le Blanc?" He hated to mention the vile man around the twins, but they needed to know too.

"We arrested him, and he's in jail under heavy guard." Bartlett sipped the hot coffee. "I've wired the district judge. I'm waiting to hear when he'll come to town to conduct the trial." He looked at the twins. "You girls haven't changed your minds about testifying against Le Blanc, have you?"

Marissa's breath came in short gasps, and her hands began to tremble. Clarissa reached over and patted her sister. "I can hardly wait. You did say he'd go to prison, didn't you? Then he couldn't come after us and punish us for testifying."

The sheriff put down the cinnamon roll. "We don't know exactly what'll happen, but with all the evidence against him, I'm sure he'll go to prison for a long time. We'll protect you from him."

Marissa sighed. Ollie glanced at his brother and found Lowell studying her. Ollie sensed his brother was as interested in Marissa as he was in Clarissa. Wouldn't it be amazing if God allowed them to marry the sisters? At least they would remain near each other. The sisters were so close that it would be a shame to separate them with much distance.

Ollie's mother gave him a sharp look, interrupting his thoughts. "Won't we, Ollie?"

Whatever it was, he knew it would be a good idea to agree with her. He nodded, wondering if he would regret it later.

His mother smiled at each young woman. "I told you that you were welcome to stay here until everything is worked out."

Yes, he could agree to that. Clarissa would be close by. He planned to get to know her well while he had the chance.

੩

They soon received word it would be the first of October before the district judge could hold court in Litchfield. Marissa was glad they'd have almost a month in this wonderful home before they had to face Pierre again. The few days they'd been there had made a big difference in how she felt about herself. Mrs. Jenson took her and Clari under her wing. She seemed to derive great pleasure from mothering them and teaching them new skills. Marissa was learning to cook. Ever since her mother died, she'd wanted to know how to bake. Although she made a big mess in the kitchen, Mrs. Jenson didn't seem to mind. She said messes were easy to clean up. She loved them the way Marissa was sure their own mother would have if she had lived.

Clari enjoyed cleaning and polishing. Mrs. Jenson said Clari's help made her work so much easier. Marissa was glad they were blending into the family so well. Several times each day, either Lowell or Ollie showed up at the house to check on them. It made Marissa feel even more special. It had been so long since she'd felt that way. She enjoyed it. She also relished every minute she spent in Lowell's company. He was quieter than his brother, but he always talked to her.

One night before falling asleep, Marissa was alone with

her thoughts. *How is it this family talks about Jesus as if He is a real person, a Friend? They mention Him so often around the table.* She recalled the service she'd attended with Pierre. She wanted to know more about this Jesus, but she hadn't the slightest idea what questions to ask.

The first Saturday evening after the twins arrived at the farm, Mrs. Jenson asked if she and her sister would like to attend church with them the next day. Marissa looked at Clari, who shrugged her shoulders.

Marissa turned back to their hostess. "We'd love to."

The next morning, she and Clari dressed with care. They wore different outfits since they didn't own two of one kind. Clari chose a silk suit in a deep, vibrant shade of blue, while Marissa wore a soft green ensemble—the one with tiny white flowers woven in. They fixed their hair in the same style, though. That way they looked alike, but their clothing matched their personalities.

Marissa thought for a moment, then turned to her sister. "I guess most of the people in Litchfield have heard about what happened the day the circus came to town. Especially since Pierre is in jail there." She hesitated. "I'm not sure what to expect from the people at church. They were friendly the other time I visited. But now I wouldn't be surprised if no one speaks to us."

"Oh, Mari, I wouldn't worry about it. If they don't speak to us now, maybe they will later. At least the Jensons do." She tucked in a stray curl, took one more look in the glass, then walked out of the room and downstairs.

Lowell and Ollie rode in the front of the two-seater surrey with the three women in back. Mrs. Jenson kept up a steady stream of conversation on the way to the church. When no one else talked, she asked questions, including all four of the young people in her comments. Marissa was glad because it helped her relax. She could sense the change in Clari too.

"Be sure to listen to what the preacher says during the service," Marissa whispered to her sister. "I want to discuss it with you later—if he preaches the way he did the other time."

When they pulled into the churchyard, people gathered around the surrey and greeted them warmly. Many asked to be introduced. Their friendliness let Marissa know they accepted her.

She hoped the preacher would talk about Jesus, and she wasn't disappointed. He preached about Jesus bringing hope and forgiveness. He mentioned some terrible sins, worse than anything she or Clari had ever done. The man said that even if a person had committed murder, Jesus would forgive him if he repented. *Repented?* That was a new word for Marissa. She planned to ask what it meant when they got home.

Clari reached over and took hold of Marissa's hand. Marissa turned to look at her sister and saw her eyes brimming with tears. During the rest of the service, they grasped each other's hands. Marissa knew they both needed what the preacher was talking about. But how did they gain that forgiveness?

At the end of the service, the pastor asked if anyone wanted to accept Jesus into his or her heart. The congregation sang a song with the phrase "O Lamb of God, I come! I come!" Marissa wanted to, but she was afraid she didn't know enough. With tears streaming down her face, she listened as everyone sang. While the pastor said the final prayer, Marissa slipped a handkerchief from her reticule and dried her cheeks. She hoped her eyes weren't too red or swollen from crying.

❧

Lowell watched Marissa throughout the service. He sensed that she was being drawn to the Savior. He prayed for her comfort and salvation. The young women needed both of these. Lowell understood what the Bible taught about a believer not marrying an unbeliever. Yet he felt such a strong pull to Marissa. His growing attraction warred with the apparent fact that she didn't know the Lord. Surely God didn't want them to turn these young women out of their home; but the longer they resided there, the more Lowell cared for Marissa. On the ride back to the house, his mother again made sure the conversation didn't lag. But he was lost in his thoughts.

At home the family sat down to the meal Mother had prepared with the help of the twins. Lowell asked a blessing on the food, and they passed the bowls filled with roast beef and vegetables around the table.

After a few moments of quiet, Lowell spoke. "Since *Far* died, we haven't had our family time in the evenings."

Ollie frowned. "We've been together."

"I guess I didn't say what I meant." Lowell cleared his throat. "We need to read the Bible together again."

His mother reached over and patted his hand. "What a wonderful idea, Lowell! I know Soren would want us to continue what he started when we first married."

That evening, after the supper dishes were cleaned up, the women joined the men in the parlor. While Lowell took out his Bible, Mrs. Jenson made room for Marissa and her sister on the settee beside her.

Lowell lowered his frame into the big chair across from the sofa, then turned to Marissa. "Where would you like me to start reading?"

ॐ

Marissa's eyes widened. Why was he asking her? She didn't know enough about the Book to tell him anything. She shrugged. "We haven't read from the Bible since our mother died, and we were very young then."

Mrs. Jenson squeezed her hand. "That's all right, Dear."

"But I do have a question—if it's all right to ask one?" Marissa felt comfortable enough with the family to assert herself.

"What would you like to know?" Lowell looked into her eyes.

"Well…this morning the preacher said something about repenting." Marissa glanced at her sister. "Clari and I don't know what that means."

Lowell gazed at her. "Do you know what sin is?"

Marissa looked down at the toe of her slipper that peeked out from under her skirt. "Yes. Most of the things Clari and I have done are sins, aren't they?" She didn't want to cry, but she couldn't keep the catch out of her voice.

"Yes, I'm afraid they are. But sin is more than that. It's anything that keeps us from doing what God wants us to do."

"How can you know what God wants you to do?" Clari's question rang through the room.

Lowell held up the Book that had been resting on his knees. "He tells us in His Word—the Bible."

Marissa glanced up. "What does that have to do with repenting?"

Lowell captured her gaze with his, then smiled, and she sensed he didn't condemn her for the things she had done. "If you choose to turn away from the sins in your life, you are repenting."

For a moment, the room was quiet while Marissa thought about what he had said. She looked at her sister. Once again, tears glistened in Clari's eyes.

"Lowell," Mrs. Jenson said, "read the Gospel of Luke,

chapter four, verse eighteen. I memorized it when I was young, and it has encouraged me many times in my life. The Lord has brought it to my mind several times since the young women have been with us. I believe it applies to them."

Lowell opened the Bible to the passage his mother had asked him to read. " 'The Spirit of the Lord is upon me, because he hath anointed me to preach the gospel to the poor; he hath sent me to heal the brokenhearted, to preach deliverance to the captives, and recovering of sight to the blind, to set at liberty them that are bruised.' Is that the verse you mean, *Mor?*"

Mrs. Jenson nodded and turned toward Marissa and Clari. "I believe Jesus wants you to know the Gospel, the good news that He came to save you from your sins. And the parts about deliverance for the captives and liberty for those who are bruised or hurt refer to what has happened in your lives."

Could it be true? Would Jesus forgive their sins and free them from hurts in their past? It was almost too much to believe. But Marissa wanted to. Tears were streaming down her cheeks too fast to wipe them off. Lowell reached into his back pocket and brought out a clean red bandanna. He handed it to her, and she started blotting her whole face.

When she looked at her sister, she was wiping her face with a matching handkerchief. Probably from Ollie. "Clari, I want what they're talking about."

"I do too." Clari turned to Mrs. Jenson. "What do we have to do?"

The older woman put her arm around her. "You just pray and tell Jesus you want Him in your life. You're ready to repent and start trusting Him, aren't you? Would you like me to help you with the prayer?" She looked from Clari to Marissa.

Both twins nodded, and Mrs. Jenson led them in a short prayer that was to the point. As Marissa said the words, she sensed a peace like nothing she'd ever felt before sweep through her. Now the tears streaming from her eyes were tears of joy. She and Clari fell into each other's arms.

"Oh, Sister!" Clari said. "Isn't it wonderful?"

Finally, Marissa pulled away and looked over at Lowell. His face was beaming, and a light shone in his eyes.

"I want to know all about Jesus!" Marissa exclaimed, and Clari nodded.

The smile on Lowell's face widened. "We'll read the Bible together every night. Then you can ask any questions you have, and we'll try to answer them."

His mother and Ollie agreed. Lowell read more from the Book then, and the words played a heavenly melody in Marissa's heart. She and Clari would have a lot to talk about when they went to their room that night.

fifteen

The Jensons had said all she had to do was repent and ask Jesus into her life.

But that's too simple, Clarissa thought later that night when she was alone. *Pierre made us steal from so many people. We'll surely have to do more than that to make up for the sins we've committed.*

But she and Mari had repeated the prayer after Mrs. Jenson anyway. She couldn't describe what washed over her then, but it took away all the dirt clinging to her soul. *I feel clean for the first time,* she marveled. *If Jesus is this powerful, I want to learn everything I can about Him.*

Each evening when the family gathered together after the meal, she drank in every word that came from that big Book and was left thirsting for more.

Lowell said he started with the Gospel of John because it told more about the life of Jesus than any other book in the Bible. On the first day, he read John, chapter one, and she and Mari found out Jesus was the Son of God, who came to live on Earth as a man. Ollie read chapter two the next day. He and Lowell planned to alternate reading the Scriptures to the family. One or more of the Jensons would eagerly answer every question Clarissa or her sister asked.

On the fourth day, Ollie read the story of the woman at the well. Clarissa felt confused by what she heard, perhaps as the Samaritan woman had been. But when Jesus told the woman about the living water, Clarissa knew that was what she and Mari were receiving each day—a drink from the fountain of living water.

On Thursday, Ollie had to pick up some supplies in Litchfield. He asked Clarissa if she and Marissa wanted to visit with Anna and Gerda while he took care of his business. They were eager to accompany him. They knew Gerda and Anna were strong Christians and wanted to share what had happened to them with their friends.

The bell over the door to the Dress Emporium brought Anna out into the shop to see who was there.

"Clarissa and Marissa!" She rushed across the store and hugged both girls at once. "Come on back to the workroom. Gerda will want to see you too."

After living out at the farm, Clarissa could see how much Anna resembled her mother. She had Mrs. Jenson's smile, and her hugs felt just as warm. Clarissa and Mari followed Anna into the back room.

"Look who I found in the front room."

Gerda glanced up from the dress she was hemming; then she quickly stood and crossed the room to hug the girls. "I'm so glad you've come to see us." She clasped her hands in front of her and looked from one to the other. "I wasn't at church the other day when you came, so now you must tell me, which one is which?"

They all laughed, then began catching up on what had been happening. Anna and Gerda had heard the general reports of how Pierre had treated his stepdaughters but not some of the particulars.

"We're so glad Ollie and Lowell rescued you." Gerda's smile was as sincere as Anna's.

Clarissa had worried about how the two women would regard them, but their openness and concern dispelled her fears. Anna and Gerda truly were their friends.

"We have something wonderful to tell you," Mari said, her eyes shining.

Anna and Gerda glanced from one twin to the other.

Clarissa smiled. "Mari had told me about going to church with Pierre some time back. That sermon made her want the forgiveness the preacher talked about, but she didn't know anything about Jesus."

"Except that He was a baby in a manger," Mari interjected.

"Then last Sunday when we both went to church, I heard about Him and wanted that same forgiveness too. After supper that night, Lowell started reading the Bible to us. We asked questions, and they all answered them for us. Then Mrs. Jenson helped us pray and ask Jesus into our lives."

"And now we're forgiven." Mari's eyes sparkled. "It's as if we're new people."

"Oh, how wonderful! That is the best news of all!" Anna wiped tears of joy from her eyes, and she and Gerda hugged the girls.

"Now every day either Ollie or Lowell reads to us from the Bible." Clarissa moved around the room as she talked. "Just last night Ollie read about the woman at the well."

"Yes, I wish I could read the story again slowly," Marissa said wistfully.

⁂

Ollie finished putting the supplies in the wagon and headed toward the dress shop. He had just entered the shop when he overheard what Marissa said. The twins didn't have a Bible. He hadn't thought about that. He left the shop and hurried into the mercantile. He stowed his purchase in the wagon, then went back to the shop to get Clarissa and her sister.

"Are you ready to go?" Ollie asked the girls.

"Oh, no, please don't take them away from us yet!" Anna turned a pleading look at him.

"I need to get back and help Lowell. We have a lot to do today."

Clarissa smiled and placed her hand on Anna's arm. "And we want to help your mother. She's been so kind to us. We're learning so much from her."

Ollie chuckled. "Besides, it's not as if you won't see them again."

On the way to the farm, Ollie could hardly hide his excitement. When would he give his present to them? As soon as they arrived or after dinner? He wasn't sure. Meanwhile, they were chattering happily about their visit. He was glad they'd enjoyed it. He hoped he could give them more happy times—especially Clarissa. The twins looked a lot alike, but he could see the subtle differences. And Clarissa was the one who tugged on his heartstrings. Now they knew the Savior. He prayed every day for the Lord to show him whether Clarissa was the woman He had chosen for him, and every day his heart drew closer to her.

Ollie managed to unload the wagon before his mother called the men into the house for dinner. He put the parcel wrapped in brown paper under his arm and dropped it behind the settee in the parlor. Maybe he would wait until the family was reading the Bible tonight.

The rest of the afternoon, while he worked, he thought about that parcel. He wondered how the young women would receive it and what their reactions would be. Family time couldn't come fast enough for him.

Finally, supper was over, and the dishes were cleaned up. Ollie sat across from the twins so he could watch their expressions while Lowell started reading the fifth chapter of John. They leaned forward on the settee, their gazes fixed on the Bible as he read, apparently listening to every word. After Lowell finished reading, first Marissa asked a question, then Clarissa. During the discussion Ollie said nothing; instead he listened and observed the girls' reactions. Finally, when the talk quieted, he stood and stretched. Then he casually walked to where he had hidden the parcel. He picked it up and laid it on the table in front of the settee.

"What's that, Son?" Mother eyed the bundle.

"It's a gift for Clarissa and Marissa."

The twins turned toward him, their eyes wide. "For us?" they exclaimed in unison.

Clarissa took the package and untied the string. The brown paper fell away, and she and her sister saw two small Bibles inside.

Clarissa looked up at him, her eyes moist. "Oh, Ollie, thank you! This is the best gift we've ever received."

Marissa smiled, her eyes moist too, and reached for one of the Books. "Yes, thank you so much, Ollie. I shall treasure this always." She ran her hand softly across the smooth leather.

Ollie continued to gaze into Clarissa's eyes. He couldn't look away if he'd wanted to, which, of course, he didn't.

❧

On the way to church on Sunday, Mrs. Jenson talked about the decision the young women had made earlier in the week. "When the pastor asks if anyone wants to accept Jesus, you can go forward and let the whole church know you've asked Him into your lives, if that's what you want to do."

Marissa smiled and nodded. "I felt a strong desire to go to the front of the church at the end of both services I've attended, but I didn't know why."

"That was the Lord calling you." Mrs. Jenson took Marissa's hand in hers. "You don't have to go forward, but the Bible does tell us that if we confess openly that Jesus is Lord and believe in our hearts that God raised Him from the dead, we'll be saved."

Lowell glanced over his shoulder at Marissa. "Pastor Harrelson may ask if you want to join the church. You might like to think about what you'll tell him."

Marissa looked at Clari. What should they tell him? Where would they be after the first of October?

Mrs. Jenson broke into Marissa's thoughts. "You don't have to join the church, if you don't want to."

"Oh, we want to, don't we, Clari?"

Clarissa nodded, and Mrs. Jenson smiled. "Then it's settled. You can join the church today."

"But we don't know where we'll be after the trial." Marissa couldn't shake this worry from her mind.

"Are you planning on going somewhere else?" Mrs. Jenson asked.

"No, but we probably need to find a job—or something."

"You'll stay with us as long as you want to. When the Lord provides something else for you, then you may go." Mrs. Jenson's declaration sounded final.

At the beginning of the service, the congregation sang "What a Friend We Have in Jesus." Marissa hadn't heard the hymn before, but it expressed her feelings exactly. No matter what happened later, she and Clari would have one special Friend who would never leave them.

≈

On Saturday, September 21, Anna Jenson and August Nilsson were married. Lowell and Ollie escorted Marissa and Clarissa to the wedding. While Anna and August repeated their vows, Lowell listened with his ears and his heart. He wanted a home and a family. Had God brought Marissa into his life for that purpose? She and her sister had traveled all over the western United States. No one had helped them find a better way of living until they visited Litchfield. Had God planned for him and his family to rescue them from their stepfather? Did He have other plans for these young women too? Was that why Lowell felt as if his heartstrings were tied to Marissa's?

He had thought she was sweet and quiet. But during the last few weeks, he had watched her spirit emerge like a butterfly from a cocoon. Her love of the Lord gave her an added peace and radiance—a radiance that was like sunshine to his heart. He didn't want to think about her ever leaving his home and family.

At the wedding reception, Lowell observed the love Anna and August showed each other. He knew in his heart he felt the same way about Marissa. Could there be a wedding in their future? When he returned home, he spent a long time on his knees seeking God's will about the relationship that had developed between them.

The next day, as they were preparing for church, Lowell didn't even hear Ollie when he asked him a question, so lost was he in his thoughts.

After dinner, Lowell and his brother set out for Ollie's half-finished house. They had agreed they needed to talk and work off some of the tension they were feeling.

"You haven't been working as diligently on the house lately, but I know you want to complete it." Lowell glanced at his brother as they rode toward the knoll.

"I've wanted to spend as much time as I could around the sisters."

Lowell smiled. "One in particular?"

Ollie laughed. "As if you didn't know!"

They dismounted and walked up the steps to the front porch. The outside walls were finished, and the roof protected the interior from the weather. Inside, though the stairs leading to the second floor were in place, many of the walls were still just studs.

"I need your help to finish this house." Ollie walked through a doorway framed in one wall. "I'm thinking about asking Clarissa to marry me." He turned to look at Lowell, who was smiling. "You're not surprised, are you?"

Lowell shoved his hands into his back pockets and rocked up on the balls of his feet. "No. I knew you were thinking about her the same way I've been thinking about Marissa. Have you prayed about it?"

Ollie rubbed the back of his neck. "It feels as if that's all I've done for a week now."

Lowell nodded but said nothing.

"I believe that's why God brought them to our town. So He could use us to rescue them—and so I could marry her."

Lowell crossed to a window and gazed out. The view from the parlor would be breathtaking, whatever the season. This would make a wonderful home for Ollie's family. "At least they would live close together." He turned to his brother. "They need to be near each other."

They shared a hearty laugh. It felt good.

"Maybe Gustaf will help us some, and even August, after he and Anna have had some time alone together. We've helped both of them when they were building. We could probably finish the inside of the house before Thanksgiving if we try."

sixteen

Tuesday, October 1, dawned clear and cool. The bright sunshine couldn't lift the gloom that had settled over Marissa, though. She dreaded this day. How could she face Pierre while she testified against him? But she knew the only way she and her sister could be free from his hold on their lives was to send him to prison for his crimes.

Marissa pictured the room full of people. The knot in her stomach tightened. She had never liked being the center of attention, and everyone at the trial would be looking at her and listening to what she said. She dropped to her knees beside the bed and poured out her heart to Jesus. A short time later she stood, walked to the washstand, and rinsed her face in the bowl of water; she felt stronger than she had in a long time.

Conversation during breakfast was light. The others must have felt the gravity of the day also. Afterward, Marissa and her sister went to their rooms to dress for court; they chose dark clothing to match their moods. Neither one fixed her hair in an elaborate style, instead pulling it back and securing it in a bun on the nape of her neck. And neither girl spoke.

Lowell and Ollie waited for them at the bottom of the stairs. Mrs. Jenson came from the kitchen to join them when they headed for the surrey. Even the trip into town was silent. The others were lost in their own thoughts, just as Marissa was in hers.

When Mother married Pierre, he had been kind to her

and Clari. She thought he would be a good stepfather. She was young enough not to know the dark side of life then. Everything around her had been bright and good. After Mother became sick, Pierre began to show his true nature, but only when Mother wasn't around. Marissa wanted to remember the good times before her mother was sick, but the recent past kept intruding on those memories.

The teacher had dismissed the students for the day so the trial could take place in the schoolhouse. The townspeople were gathered in small clusters in front of the building, talking. Marissa looked away, then closed her eyes and prayed before Lowell helped her alight from the surrey.

Inside the schoolhouse, Pierre sat at a table near the front, but he was turned toward the door. Marissa tried to look away, but his gaze locked with hers, sending cold chills down her spine. He studied her, as a rattlesnake studies its prey before striking. She could see his hands clenched into tight fists at his side, as they had been in the past before he struck her. Her breath came in short gasps. She felt something almost tangible reaching out from him to pull her back into his grasp. He mouthed some words at her. They looked like, *I'll get you for this.*

Marissa looked at Clari. Her face had paled to the color of chalk. Her eyes wide with fear, she grasped her hands so tightly her knuckles had become white. Marissa wanted to flee from that room and never look back. But she couldn't. She had to testify. She had to tell the truth, despite the conflict raging inside her.

Lowell slipped his arm around her waist and pulled her close to his side. He leaned down and whispered into her ear, " 'I can do all things through Christ which strengtheneth me.' "

Marissa had never read that passage, but she knew it had to be from the Bible. Jesus would give her strength. She held her head high and walked with Lowell to the seats the sheriff had saved for them.

The judge entered the room, and everyone rose until he was settled behind the table in the front. Marissa studied his face. He appeared solemn, but laugh lines around his eyes and mouth indicated he wasn't always that way. He looked at her just then and smiled. She took a deep breath and fixed her gaze on the judge.

Marissa had always feared anyone connected with the law because she was guilty of doing what Pierre had forced her to. The judge knew what she had done. In fact, Lowell had told her that the judge knew everything about the case before it started. The man smiled at her again, as a loving father might smile upon his daughter. She could do what she needed to.

The judge pounded his gavel on the table, and sudden quiet filled the room. It didn't take long for Sheriff Bartlett to present his case. Three deputies told about capturing Pierre with the stolen goods. Then came Marissa's turn to answer questions. Clari would testify last. Before Marissa arose to take the stand, Lowell gave her hand a squeeze. "I'll be praying for you," he whispered.

Marissa decided not to look at Pierre. Instead she focused on the man asking the questions and answered every question with the truth.

❧

Lowell's heart pounded in his ears as he watched Marissa approach the witness chair. He hated for her to go up there alone; he knew how difficult it was for her. He could only pray for her strength during the questioning. When she finished, he whispered a prayer of thanks. He wanted to protect her, with his own life if need be. Gud, *I love her with my whole heart. Help me know what You want me to do.* A sense of peace enveloped him.

Marissa finished her testimony and returned to her chair. Lowell stood, took her arm, and escorted her from the courtroom.

"Don't I need to stay?" she asked when they were outside the schoolhouse.

"No. You've done your part. Let's go for a walk."

"What if Clari needs me?"

"She'll do fine. Besides Ollie will be there for her."

At first they walked in silence, and Lowell held her hand. He wanted to comfort her and never let her go. He guided her away from the crowd to a small park nestled among tall trees. They found a bench and sat quietly for a time. Lowell sensed a great peace surrounding them. Only the birds chirping overhead broke the stillness.

Marissa turned her face toward him and smiled. It was such a sweet smile that he wanted to take her in his arms.

"Marissa, do you have any idea how I feel about you?"

She lowered her gaze to their hands clasped on the bench between them. "I. . .I'm not sure, Lowell, but I'd like to know."

"You're very important to me." He drew her into his arms and rested his chin on the top of her head. "I want to protect you from anything that might hurt you."

She nestled close against his chest. "I'm sure you could," she whispered, then looked up into his eyes.

Lowell's face drifted closer to hers until their lips touched. He felt such a sweet, tender connection between them. Warmth flooded his body. He pulled away and took a deep breath.

"We need to get back and see what the verdict is."

❧

Ollie felt great relief when the trial ended. The judge and jury had been appalled when they heard what Clarissa and her sister had gone through. Because of the evidence and the girls' testimonies, the jury was quick to give Pierre a life sentence. Ollie was glad Lowell had taken Marissa out of the courtroom. When Pierre heard the verdict, his outburst was loud and ugly. Ollie wished Clarissa hadn't heard it, either. The man's vindictive words must have wounded her deeply. The judge immediately restored order to the court, and the U.S. marshal and his deputies led Pierre away in handcuffs. The twins would never have to see him again.

Ollie glanced at Sheriff Bartlett, who nodded. Ollie slipped his arm under Clarissa's and quietly escorted her out the back door before the judge dismissed everyone. He wanted to spare her from the crowds. They walked up the street, hunting for Lowell and Marissa. Finally, they gave up when they reached the church.

Clarissa looked at the open door. "Do you think it would be all right to go inside? I mean, it isn't Sunday, after all."

Ollie smiled at her. "Sure. We can go in anytime. It's the Lord's house, you know."

They walked up to the front pew and sat down. Clarissa bowed her head.

"Dear Jesus, thank You for helping Mari and me get through the trial. Thank You for giving us strength to help put Pierre in prison where he belongs. And thank You for sending Ollie and Lowell to rescue us from him. Amen."

Ollie kept his head bowed after she finished. Her prayer echoed his own thoughts. But he also sent one more silent plea toward heaven.

As they made their way to the back of the church, Ollie reached out and drew Clarissa into his arms. She gazed up at him, and the desire to kiss her lips overcame him. He lowered his head, then hesitated. He wanted to give her a chance to turn away. Instead she closed the distance between them. Her mouth tasted like honey to him, and he wanted to hold her in his arms forever.

He pulled back, then settled her closer into his arms. "Oh, Clarissa, what am I going to do about you?"

⁊⊷

Back at the farm, the sisters went to their rooms to change clothes. Lowell and Ollie followed their mother into the kitchen.

Lowell crossed his arms and leaned against the counter. *"Moder,* we want to ask you something."

She turned around and smiled, waiting for him to continue.

Lowell stood up straight and stuck his hands in his back pockets. Why was he nervous? He should be able to say what was on his mind.

"I want to ask Marissa to marry me." He felt better after the words were out.

Ollie stepped up beside him. "And I want to marry Clarissa."

Mother smiled. "I'm not surprised."

Lowell rubbed his hands on his trousers. Why were his palms sweating? "Is that all right with you?"

Mother laughed. "I would love to have them in the family. They seem like daughters to me already. And they need a family to love them."

Lowell grinned. He felt like shouting. Ollie turned and strode from the room. Lowell could hear the barn door slamming shut, then the faint sound of a joyous whoop.

"What's wrong with Ollie?" Clarissa had just come into the kitchen.

Lowell laughed. "I don't know. Why don't you go see about him?"

"Is anyone going to tell me what's going on?" Marissa asked.

Lowell and his mother laughed, and Marissa raised her brows. A puzzled look was on her face. Maybe he was crazy. Crazy in love.

❧

Clarissa stepped through the barn door. "Oh, there you are, Ollie. Are you all right?"

"Sure. How about if we take a ride after lunch? I'd like to show you something."

"What is it?"

Ollie smiled, his eyes twinkling. "Oh, you'll see." He smiled again.

After lunch, Mrs. Jenson told her and Mari they didn't need to help with the dishes, but they insisted. When they finished, the surrey and two other horses stood in front of the house. Ollie had suggested Clarissa put on a riding skirt so she dashed upstairs, changed, then hurried back down. Lowell was escorting Mari to the surrey. Ollie had saddled a gentle mare for Clarissa to ride. He boosted her up, then mounted his own horse.

They started across the pasture. Soon they came to a house sitting on a hill. Ollie stopped in front of it and dismounted. He helped her down from her horse, then pulled her into his arms and kissed the top of her head. A shiver coursed through her. She had never felt like this before.

"Are you cold?" he whispered against her hair.

"No." She looked up into his eyes. The clear green deepened as his gaze intensified.

She was quiet for a moment, then asked, "Whose house is this?"

Ollie cleared his throat and led her by the hand up the steps to the front porch. "It's mine, but it isn't finished."

He opened the door, and Clarissa stepped through into what looked like a dream world to her. She knew the house wasn't finished, but she could picture beautiful wallpaper with tiny flowers, pictures of lovely scenes on the walls, a fire in the fireplace, and lace curtains at the windows. How she wished she could live in such a house.

Ollie placed his hands lightly on her shoulders and turned her toward him. "And it can be your home, if you'll marry me."

Clarissa caught her breath. Had he asked her to marry him? Were her dreams coming true? Tears filled her eyes.

He gently cupped her cheeks in his strong palms. "Please don't cry. I love you."

"But they're tears of joy, Ollie. I've never been so happy." It was hard to get the words past the lump in her throat.

"Then are you saying yes?" He held his breath.

Clarissa nodded and stood on tiptoe to touch his lips briefly with hers, but he captured her in an embrace that made her feel protected and cherished. The kiss deepened, and her insides felt molten. She could hardly believe this man loved her, and she was going to spend the rest of her life with him. God had been so good to her.

❧

Marissa had looked back at Ollie as she and Lowell drove away in the surrey. He was taking Clari riding. Maybe the brothers wanted to help Marissa and her sister celebrate the end of Pierre's hold on their lives. It felt odd to ride in the middle of the day. No one had done any chores before the trial, so she thought the men would need to work when they returned home.

Marissa looked at Lowell. "Where are we going?"

"I thought you might want to go for a ride." He pulled her close to him and kept his arm around her. "I know a place by a stream where we can sit and talk."

Marissa liked sitting nestled close to him. If only it didn't have to end. She would be happy to spend the rest of her life with Lowell, but she knew that was unreasonable. She knew he liked her a lot, but she wished it were more than that. Marissa wasn't sure when she had started loving him, but she had been drawn to him as long as she'd known him. It was only a few months, but it seemed much longer than that. She felt as if her life began when she met him.

Lowell pulled the surrey off the road and parked it under a grove of trees. He helped her alight and led her deeper into the grove. Soon she heard the sound of water gurgling over rocks. The sun shone through the branches above the brook, and sparkles danced on the surface of the water. What a beautiful place!

Lowell stuffed his hands in his back pockets, then pulled them out. She had seen him do this many times, but it was usually when he was nervous. What did he have to be nervous about? She studied his expression. Whatever was on his mind was important.

She touched his arm. "What's the matter, Lowell? Can I help?"

He took her hands in his. "Yes, you can. You can marry me."

Marissa looked at him thoughtfully. "Why do you want me to marry you?" She hoped it wasn't because he felt sorry for her and Clari because they had no home.

He gathered her gently in his arms. "I'm not doing this very well, am I?" He rested his chin on the top of her head. "Marissa, I love you so much it hurts. I can't imagine my life without you in it."

She smiled and looked up at him. "I love you too, Lowell. And I want to marry you."

She placed her hand on his cheek. He had no doubt shaved that morning, but she could feel a tiny bit of stubble against her palm. His masculinity made her feel safe.

He lowered his head until his lips touched hers. This time he didn't pull away quickly. His kiss awakened every part of her being. The thought that she could experience kisses like this for the rest of her life washed over her, and she poured her love into returning his kiss.

epilogue

They had chosen the Saturday after Thanksgiving for the wedding day. The dreams Marissa and Clarissa had shared in the forest were coming true. They would have a double wedding, and Lowell and Ollie were the grooms. Mrs. Jenson had offered to move to town and live with Gerda over the Dress Emporium, but neither of the twins would hear of it. Marissa wanted her mother-in-law to continue living in the home she had shared with her husband. She knew she would need the older woman's help. She hadn't learned all she needed to know about running a household and being a wife. Clarissa assured Mrs. Jenson she would need her help too.

Ollie and Clarissa's house was finished, but all the furniture they'd ordered hadn't arrived yet. They would move in right after the wedding, but it would take awhile before the household was settled.

The day of the wedding was a winter spectacle. It had snowed earlier in the week, and the sun on the white expanse lent a special glow to the bare tree branches encased in ice. Everything sparkled as if celebrating the special day.

Anna and Gerda came to the farm to help the sisters don the dresses they had made for them. They had created the same style but in different fabrics. Marissa wore a pure white brocade and Clarissa a rich cream-colored satin.

August brought a sleigh to take the brides to the wedding. The girls had never ridden in a sleigh and laughed all the way to the church. The horses wore bells on their harnesses, and the merry jingling was the perfect accompaniment to the excitement Clarissa and Marissa felt. The church was filled when they arrived, and some people had even clustered around the doors.

Mrs. Olson played the pump organ while Gustaf escorted Marissa down the aisle to Lowell. Then August walked with Clarissa to Ollie. In their dreams, this had been a fairy-tale ending for the girls' lives, but they both realized this was truly the beginning—of a more wonderful life than either had ever imagined—a life free from deception.

A Letter To Our Readers

Dear Reader:

In order that we might better contribute to your reading enjoyment, we would appreciate your taking a few minutes to respond to the following questions. We welcome your comments and read each form and letter we receive. When completed, please return to the following:

Fiction Editor
Heartsong Presents
PO Box 719
Uhrichsville, Ohio 44683

1. Did you enjoy reading *Double Deception* by Lena Nelson Dooley?
❏ Very much! I would like to see more books by this author!
❏ Moderately. I would have enjoyed it more if

_____

_____

_____

2. Are you a member of **Heartsong Presents**? ❏ Yes ❏ No
If no, where did you purchase this book? _____

_____

3. How would you rate, on a scale from 1 (poor) to 5 (superior), the cover design? _____

4. On a scale from 1 (poor) to 10 (superior), please rate the following elements.

____ Heroine   ____ Plot
____ Hero   ____ Inspirational theme
____ Setting   ____ Secondary characters

5. These characters were special because?_____

_____

_____

6. How has this book inspired your life?_____

_____

_____

7. What settings would you like to see covered in future
   Heartsong Presents books? _____

_____

_____

8. What are some inspirational themes you would like to see
   treated in future books? _____

_____

_____

9. Would you be interested in reading other **Heartsong
   Presents** titles? ❏ Yes ❏ No

10. Please check your age range:
   ❏ Under 18   ❏ 18-24
   ❏ 25-34   ❏ 35-45
   ❏ 46-55   ❏ Over 55

Name_____

Occupation _____

Address _____

City_____ State_____ Zip_____

Alaskan
MIDNIGHT

4 stories in 1

Four women head to Juneau, Alaska, hoping to stitch a new section in their life quilts—a more beautiful section without the tearstains of the past.

Author Joyce Livingston blends the charm of quilting, the drama of the Alaskan landscape, and the thrill of romance into four modern stories of faith and healing.

Historical, paperback, 464 pages, 5 ³/₁₆"x 8"

❤ ❤ ❤ ❤ ❤ ❤ ❤ ❤ ❤ ❤ ❤ ❤ ❤ ❤ ❤

❤ ❤ ❤ ❤ ❤ ❤ ❤ ❤ ❤ ❤ ❤ ❤ ❤ ❤ ❤

Hearts♥ng

Any 12 Heartsong Presents titles for only $27.00*

HISTORICAL ROMANCE IS CHEAPER BY THE DOZEN!

Buy any assortment of twelve *Heartsong Presents* titles and save 25% off of the already discounted price of $2.97 each!

*plus $2.00 shipping and handling per order and sales tax where applicable.

HEARTSONG PRESENTS TITLES AVAILABLE NOW:

Presents

Great Inspirational Romance at a Great Price!

Heartsong Presents books are inspirational romances in contemporary and historical settings, designed to give you an enjoyable, spirit-lifting reading experience. You can choose wonderfully written titles from some of today's best authors like Peggy Darty, Sally Laity, Tracie Peterson, Colleen L. Reece, Debra White Smith, and many others.

When ordering quantities less than twelve, above titles are $2.97 each.
Not all titles may be available at time of order.